The North Pole Diaries Secrets of Santa's Workshop

Freya Jobe

Published by Freya Jobe, 2024.

This is a work of fiction. Similarities to real people, places, or events are entirely coincidental.

THE NORTH POLE DIARIES SECRETS OF SANTA'S WORKSHOP

First edition. November 18, 2024.

Copyright © 2024 Freya Jobe.

ISBN: 979-8230579038

Written by Freya Jobe.

The North Pole Diaries
Secrets of Santa's Workshop

Welcome to the North Pole, where snow falls endlessly, candy canes grow like wildflowers, and Christmas magic is made around the clock. It might seem like a perfect winter wonderland from the outside, but behind the twinkling lights and jolly music lies a bustling workshop filled with personalities, problems, and, yes, plenty of laughs.

This book offers an exclusive, behind-the-scenes peek into the daily lives of Santa, Mrs. Claus, the elves, and even the reindeer—all through their personal diary entries. Think of it as the North Pole's tell-all journal, where secrets, mishaps, and heartfelt moments are scribbled down for you to enjoy.

You'll discover that even Santa forgets where he left his glasses, Mrs. Claus occasionally burns her famous cookies, and the elves sometimes debate the merits of glitter way more than they should. It's not always smooth sailing in the workshop, but through the chaos, the laughter, and the snowball fights, one thing remains true: everyone here is united by their love for Christmas.

Each story is a short diary entry from a different character's perspective, revealing their quirks, worries, and triumphs as they prepare for the most magical day of the year. Whether it's an elf trying to win the annual gingerbread contest or Rudolph navigating life in the spotlight, these pages are filled with humour, heart, and just a sprinkle of holiday mishaps.

So grab a cup of cocoa, cozy up by the fire, and get ready to laugh, smile, and feel the magic of Christmas like never before. Because even at the North Pole, life isn't perfect—it's just perfectly wonderful.

Welcome to the diaries. Let the merriment begin!

Chapter 1: Monday Morning Madness

Diary of Santa Claus, December 1st, 8:00 AM

It finally happened. For the first time in centuries, I overslept. Mrs. Claus warned me last night not to finish that extra slice of peppermint pie, but did I listen? No. The sugar crash hit hard, and I slept through my alarm clock—twice. Now, here I am, groggily pulling on my boots while the workshop descends into absolute chaos. The elves are trying to keep the morning schedule on track without me, but judging by the clanging noises and occasional yells, it's not going well.

Diary of Jingle the Elf, 8:15 AM

"Where's Santa?" I asked Sparkle as I passed her on the conveyor belt line. She was knee-deep in plush reindeer toys, frantically stitching antlers onto heads.

"I don't know, but he's late!" she replied, her voice muffled by the thread she held between her teeth.

By now, word had spread across the workshop: Santa wasn't in his office. Santa wasn't inspecting the sleigh. Santa wasn't anywhere. It was as if the big guy had vanished into thin air, leaving us to fend for ourselves.

Diary of Sparkle the Elf, 8:30 AM

I've never seen anything like it. The toy assembly line came to a screeching halt when Grizzle tried to "take charge" in Santa's absence. Let's just say that organization isn't his strong suit. Within minutes, there were teddy bear arms flying in one direction and mismatched doll heads in another.

"Everyone, calm down!" Grizzle bellowed, waving his clipboard like a sword.

"Calm down?!" shouted Tinsel from the paint station. "Do you know how many orders we have to complete by noon?"

Grizzle ignored her and started assigning random tasks. He put Sprinkle, who usually works on train sets, in charge of assembling electronics. Big mistake. Five minutes later, she somehow managed to make a tablet play "Jingle Bells" in reverse at full volume.

Diary of Rudolph, 9:00 AM

The commotion woke me up from a delightful nap in the stables. At first, I thought it was just the usual Monday morning chaos. But when Prancer burst in and declared, "Santa's missing!" I knew something serious was going on.

We reindeer may not handle the toys, but without Santa, our training schedule is thrown completely off. I trotted over to the workshop to investigate and immediately regretted it. The place looked like a snowstorm hit it—complete with glitter clouds and candy cane shrapnel.

"Who's in charge here?" I asked.

Grizzle puffed out his chest. "Me."

I couldn't help but laugh. "Good luck with that."

Diary of Mrs. Claus, 9:15 AM

I knew something was wrong when I woke up to the sound of distant shouting. Normally, Santa is up before the sun, bustling about with a cup of cocoa and that ridiculous checklist of his. But this morning, the only thing bustling was the chaos in the workshop.

When I found Santa still snoring in bed, I nearly dropped my rolling pin. "Nicholas!" I said, shaking him awake.

"Huh? What time is it?" he mumbled, sitting up with a groggy look.

"Time for you to get to work! The elves are losing their minds!"

That got him moving. He leapt out of bed and fumbled with his coat, muttering something about how he "never should've had that third helping."

Diary of Tinsel the Elf, 9:30 AM

By the time Mrs. Claus showed up, the workshop looked like a war zone. Half the elves were arguing over who should be in charge, while the other half were trying to salvage what they could from the assembly line.

"Enough!" Mrs. Claus shouted, her voice cutting through the chaos like a whip. "Everyone back to your stations! Santa will be here shortly."

Her calm authority restored a little order, but just as things started to settle down, the conveyor belt jolted to life again—and promptly spat out a teddy bear with three ears.

"Great," I muttered. "We're doomed."

Diary of Santa Claus, 9:45 AM

When I finally made it to the workshop, the first thing I saw was Grizzle perched on a stack of toy boxes, barking orders like a drill sergeant. The second thing I saw was a life-sized doll missing half its face. And the third thing I saw was Mrs. Claus, hands on her hips, glaring at me like I'd forgotten our anniversary.

"Care to explain?" she asked.

"Peppermint pie," I muttered sheepishly.

She shook her head. "Get to work, Nicholas."

Diary of Jingle the Elf, 10:00 AM

Santa's arrival was met with a collective sigh of relief. Within minutes, he had the conveyor belts running smoothly again, reassigned everyone to their proper stations, and even managed to fix the glitchy tablet Sprinkle had messed up.

But the highlight of the morning? When Santa climbed onto the platform, cleared his throat, and said, "I'm sorry, everyone. I overslept."

You could've heard a snowflake drop. Santa? Oversleep? It was like finding out reindeer can't actually fly.

Then he smiled and added, "I guess even Santa needs a day off now and then, huh?"

We all laughed, and just like that, the tension melted away.

Diary of Sparkle the Elf, 10:30 AM

With Santa back in charge, the workshop returned to its usual organized chaos. By noon, we were back on schedule, and the three-eared teddy bears had been replaced with proper ones.

Still, I can't help but wonder—what would we do if Santa didn't wake up one day? Maybe we should invest in a second-in-command. Definitely not Grizzle, though.

Diary of Mrs. Claus, 11:00 AM

After everything settled down, I brought Santa a fresh cup of cocoa and sat with him in his office. He looked tired but relieved.

"Do you think the elves will forgive me?" he asked, sipping his drink.

I patted his hand. "Of course they will. But next time, Nicholas, maybe listen to me about that second slice of pie."

He chuckled and gave me a sheepish grin. "Point taken."

Diary of Santa Claus, 11:30 AM

As the morning chaos fades into memory, I can't help but feel grateful. Yes, I overslept. Yes, the workshop nearly fell apart without me. But in the end, we pulled through—together.

That's the magic of the North Pole. No matter how messy things get, we always find a way to make it work. And as I look out my window at the bustling workshop below, I know one thing for sure: Christmas is back on track.

Now, if you'll excuse me, I have a tray of Mrs. Claus's cookies waiting for me. Maybe just one this time.

Or two.

Chapter 2: Mrs. Claus's Cookie Crisis

Diary of Mrs. Claus, December 3rd, 7:00 AM

It's cookie day! Every December 3rd, I whip up batch after batch of my famous sugar cookies to keep the elves energized and spirits high. I've been making these cookies for centuries, and they're a highlight of the season. Santa claims they're the reason he can get through December without losing his jolly demeanour.

I've got my apron on, my mixing bowls ready, and enough sugar to build an igloo. Well, I thought I did. The sugar bin felt suspiciously light this morning. No matter—I'll make it work. After all, Christmas is all about improvisation, isn't it?

Diary of Jingle the Elf, 8:30 AM

The workshop smelled amazing this morning. Mrs. Claus's cookies are legendary around here. We'd barely started working when she arrived with a fresh tray, her cheeks rosy, her apron dusted with flour.

"Cookies are ready!" she sang.

The elves cheered and swarmed the tray like reindeer to a hay bale. I snagged one, eager for the first bite. But as soon as I took a nibble, my taste buds screamed in protest.

Salt.

Lots of salt.

My entire mouth felt like I'd licked an icicle dipped in seawater. I glanced around to see if anyone else noticed, and judging by the horrified expressions, I wasn't alone.

"Delicious as always, Mrs. Claus!" Sparkle said, forcing a smile as she took another bite.

Diary of Sparkle the Elf, 8:45 AM

I couldn't do it. I couldn't tell Mrs. Claus the truth. She looked so proud standing there, waiting for our feedback, her eyes twinkling like the northern lights.

"Best batch yet!" I blurted out, hoping no one would contradict me.

Mrs. Claus beamed. "Oh, you're too kind, Sparkle! There's plenty more where that came from."

The moment she left, Jingle leaned over and whispered, "What was that? Salt cookies?"

I nodded grimly. "I think she mixed up the sugar and salt."

"What do we do?" he asked, eyeing the remaining cookies on the tray.

"Eat them. Smile. Pretend they're great," I said, shoving the rest of mine into my mouth with a dramatic grimace.

Diary of Mrs. Claus, 9:00 AM

I knew they'd love them! The elves gobbled up the first tray so quickly that I rushed back to the kitchen to bake more. Nothing makes me happier than seeing them enjoy my cookies while they work. I'll make an extra batch for Santa. He always says my cookies are better than his cocoa.

Diary of Santa Claus, 9:30 AM

"Cookies!" Mrs. Claus announced, setting down a plate on my desk with a flourish.

"Ah, my favorite part of the season," I said, grabbing one. But the moment I bit into it, I knew something was wrong. The saltiness hit me like a snowball to the face. I chewed slowly, trying to mask my reaction.

"What do you think?" she asked, watching me expectantly.

"Wonderful, as always," I said, doing my best to sound convincing. "A unique twist this year!"

Her face lit up. "You noticed! I'm experimenting a little. I'll bring more later."

Oh, no.

Diary of Tinsel the Elf, 10:00 AM

Word spread fast: the cookies were terrible, but no one had the heart to tell Mrs. Claus. By mid-morning, we had a mountain of untouched cookies piling up in the breakroom. The reindeer even refused to eat them, and they've been known to eat pinecones.

"What do we do?" Jingle whispered.

"We can't hurt her feelings," I said. "She's worked so hard."

"But if she keeps baking, we'll drown in salt cookies!"

I sighed. "Let's just hope someone braver than us breaks the news."

Diary of Rudolph, 10:30 AM

When I saw the plate of cookies in the stable, I got excited. Mrs. Claus's cookies are usually the highlight of my day. But as soon as I took a bite, I realized something was horribly wrong.

"What is this?" Blitzen asked, spitting crumbs into the hay.

"Maybe it's a new recipe?" I offered, not wanting to hurt her feelings.

Dasher shook his head. "If she brings more, we have to tell her. We can't let this continue."

"Are you volunteering?" I asked.

Dasher snorted. "Not a chance."

Diary of Mrs. Claus, 11:00 AM

I decided to bring another batch to the workshop. The elves have been working so hard, and they deserve a little treat.

When I walked in, though, I noticed something strange. The cookie trays I'd brought earlier were still half full. Normally, the cookies disappear in minutes. Maybe I overestimated how many they'd want?

"Everything okay?" I asked.

Jingle nodded furiously. "Oh, yes! We're just... pacing ourselves!"

Sparkle chimed in. "They're so good we want to make them last!"

How sweet.

Diary of Jingle the Elf, 11:15 AM

We're doomed. Mrs. Claus saw the uneaten cookies and got worried we weren't eating enough. Now she's planning to bake even more.

"This can't go on," I whispered to Sparkle.

"But who's going to tell her?" she whispered back.

Just then, Santa walked into the workshop, chewing on one of the cookies. He gave us a pained look as he approached. "So... how are you all enjoying Mrs. Claus's latest batch?"

"We're trying," I said.

"Good. Keep trying," he replied with a grim nod.

Diary of Mrs. Claus, 11:45 AM

Something feels off. Santa barely finished his cookie at lunch, and the elves didn't cheer when I brought in the latest tray. Usually, they can't get enough of my cookies.

Could it be? Did I make a mistake?

I checked my recipe and stared at the salt jar sitting on the counter. A sinking feeling hit me. Oh no.

Diary of Tinsel the Elf, 12:00 PM

Mrs. Claus called an emergency meeting in the workshop. We all gathered nervously, unsure what to expect.

"I have a confession to make," she said, holding up a jar of salt. "I think I mixed this up with the sugar."

The room fell silent. Then, to everyone's surprise, Santa started laughing.

"It happens to the best of us," he said. "Remember the time I spilled cocoa all over the Naughty List?"

The elves chuckled, and the tension melted away.

Mrs. Claus looked relieved. "Why didn't anyone tell me?"

We exchanged sheepish glances. "We didn't want to hurt your feelings," Jingle admitted.

"Well," she said, smiling, "next time, be honest. Now, who wants to help me bake a proper batch?"

Diary of Sparkle the Elf, 1:00 PM

Crisis averted. Mrs. Claus's new batch of cookies was perfect, and the workshop smelled amazing again. As we devoured the fresh cookies, she joked, "I think I'll label my jars from now on."

We all laughed, and Santa gave her a warm hug. "You're still the best baker in the North Pole, salt or no salt."

And just like that, everything felt right again.

Diary of Mrs. Claus, 2:00 PM

Mistakes happen, even in the North Pole. But I'm lucky to have such kind-hearted elves and a husband who always knows how to make me smile. The important thing is that the cookies are back to their usual sugary goodness, and Christmas is still on track.

Now, if I could just figure out why the reindeer are avoiding the stable...

Chapter 3: Diary of a Grumpy Elf

Diary of Grizzle the Elf, December 4th, 6:00 AM

Here we go again. Another day at the workshop, another day stuck doing the worst job in existence: toy inspection. While everyone else gets to assemble cool gadgets, paint colorful toys, or stuff teddy bears with fluffy cotton, I'm stuck with the rejects.

Broken toys, faulty gadgets, and mismatched parts—it's like Christmas' dumpster fire, and I'm the poor soul tasked with sifting through it. I keep telling the Head Elf I'd be much better suited to toy design, but noooo, "Grizzle, you're so meticulous! You're perfect for quality control."

Meticulous? Try miserable.

Diary of Grizzle the Elf, 7:30 AM

First toy of the day: a jack-in-the-box. Simple enough, right? Wrong. The spring inside was so tight that when I cranked the handle, the clown shot out like a rocket and hit me square in the face. Great start.

Second toy: a remote-control car. Except the remote didn't control the car; it controlled the sleigh parked in the corner. Poor Jingle was nearly run over.

By the third toy—a doll that only said "Help!" when you pulled the string—I seriously started to wonder if the toys were cursed.

Diary of Jingle the Elf, 8:00 AM

Grizzle is in one of his moods again. You can hear him muttering from across the workshop. I get it—toy inspection isn't the most glamorous job. But somebody has to do it!

When I brought him a tray of cocoa to cheer him up, he just glared at me.

"Let me guess," he said, eyeing the tray. "You want me to inspect this for marshmallow quality, too?"

"Come on, Grizzle," I said. "It's not that bad."

He raised an eyebrow and held up a teddy bear missing both eyes. "Tell that to Cyclops Bear here."

I left before he could throw it at me.

Diary of Grizzle the Elf, 9:15 AM

Another hour, another parade of disasters. Here's the rundown: A train set that only goes in reverse.

A stuffed penguin with one flipper sewn on its head.

A toy trumpet that sounds like a foghorn.

And the pièce de résistance? A dollhouse that bursts into flames when you open the front door. I'm pretty sure we're violating some kind of safety code here.

Diary of Sparkle the Elf, 9:30 AM

Grizzle stomped into the breakroom muttering about "dollhouse arson" and "jack-in-the-box warfare." He grabbed a cookie, shoved it into his mouth, and sat down with a huff.

"Why don't you ask to be reassigned?" I asked.

He glared at me. "You think I haven't tried? Every time I bring it up, the Head Elf says I'm too 'valuable' in toy inspection. Valuable? More like expendable!"

"Maybe if you had a more positive attitude..."

"Positive attitude?" he snapped. "Would you be positive if you had to inspect a pogo stick that doubles as a flamethrower?"

I decided to leave him alone.

Diary of Grizzle the Elf, 10:00 AM

The Head Elf came by for one of his "pep talks." Spoiler alert: they don't work.

"Grizzle," he said, clapping me on the back, "you're doing an important job! Without you, these faulty toys could end up in children's hands on Christmas morning."

"Great," I said. "So I'm the last line of defence in preventing Christmas catastrophes. No pressure."

He laughed, like I was joking.

"Keep up the good work!" he said, strolling away.
I glared at his retreating back. "Oh, I'll keep it up. Until I lose my sanity."

Diary of Dasher, 10:30 AM
We reindeer don't usually get involved in elf business, but even I've noticed Grizzle's bad mood. He stormed into the stables earlier, muttering something about "a cursed assembly line" and "being the only competent elf in the workshop."

"Rough day?" I asked.

He snorted. "Every day is rough when you're stuck with defective pogo sticks and exploding dollhouses."

I tried to cheer him up. "At least you're not the one flying through a snowstorm on Christmas Eve."

He shot me a look. "I'd trade places with you in a heartbeat."

I decided not to push my luck.

Diary of Grizzle the Elf, 11:00 AM
If one more elf tells me to "look on the bright side," I'm going to lose it. The bright side of what? Spending my days surrounded by toys that seem determined to destroy me?

Just now, I tested a drum set that played "Jingle Bells" at ear-splitting volume. The sound was so loud it shattered every snow globe in the room. Of course, that led to another lecture from the Head Elf about "handling toys with care."

I don't get paid enough for this. Actually, I don't get paid at all.

Diary of Sparkle the Elf, 11:45 AM
Grizzle was still sulking when Mrs. Claus showed up with a tray of freshly baked cookies. She handed him one and said, "I hear you've been working hard, Grizzle. Thank you for all that you do."

He grumbled something under his breath but took the cookie.

"You know," she said, sitting down beside him, "not everyone can do what you do. You have a sharp eye, and that's what makes you so good at toy inspection. You're making Christmas better for every child out there."

For a moment, I thought I saw him smile.

Diary of Grizzle the Elf, 12:30 PM

Fine. I'll admit it: Mrs. Claus has a point.

I don't love toy inspection. In fact, I hate it. But when I think about some kid waking up on Christmas morning to find a perfect teddy bear or a working train set under the tree, I guess it's worth it.

That doesn't mean I'm going to stop complaining, though. Complaining is part of who I am.

Diary of Santa Claus, 1:00 PM

Mrs. Claus told me about Grizzle's bad day, so I stopped by the toy inspection station to check on him.

"How's it going, Grizzle?" I asked.

He held up a pogo stick with a bent spring. "Living the dream, Santa."

I chuckled. "I know it's not glamorous, but you're one of the most important elves here. You're the reason Christmas morning is magical for so many kids."

He muttered something about "pressure" and went back to work, but I could tell he appreciated it.

Diary of Grizzle the Elf, 2:00 PM

Santa stopped by earlier to thank me. That's the thing about him—he's always so... jolly. It's hard to stay grumpy when he's around.

After he left, I found a note tucked into my toolbox. It said, "To the best toy inspector in the North Pole—thank you for making Christmas magic happen."

Okay, fine. Maybe today wasn't so bad after all.

Diary of Jingle the Elf, 3:00 PM

Grizzle actually smiled today. It was brief, but it happened. Mrs. Claus's cookies and Santa's pep talk must have worked.

"Feeling better?" I asked.

He shrugged. "A little."

I handed him a teddy bear with a missing nose. "Well, if you're up for it, we could use your expertise on this one."

He rolled his eyes but grabbed his tools. "Let's fix it."

Diary of Grizzle the Elf, 5:00 PM

The day is over, and I survived.

I'm still not thrilled about toy inspection, but I guess it's not the worst job in the world. At least I'm good at it. And if my work makes Christmas a little brighter for kids everywhere, maybe it's worth the headache.

Just don't expect me to stop grumbling. After all, I'm Grizzle the Grumpy Elf. It's kind of my thing.

Chapter 4: Rudolph's Red-Nose Remedy

The North Pole was in full holiday swing, with the workshop bustling, the elves chattering, and the faint scent of peppermint wafting through the air. But in the reindeer stables, things were far from merry. Reindeer flu had struck again—a dreaded annual occurrence that turned even the mightiest fliers into sneezing, sniffling wrecks.

For Rudolph, the season was particularly challenging. His legendary glowing nose, the very symbol of Christmas miracles, became both a blessing and a curse during flu season. The glow wasn't just a handy fog light; it also drew constant attention to his sniffles, making him the unwilling star of the North Pole infirmary.

"Rudolph, hold still," Dr. Fawn said, prodding at his glowing nose with a thermometer. "Your temperature's fine, but this redness is—well—extra red."

"It's always red," Rudolph muttered, his voice nasally from congestion.

"Yes, but now it's glowing like a full-blown lighthouse," she said, jotting notes on her clipboard.

"It's the flu," Rudolph groaned. "It always happens. The more I sneeze, the brighter it gets."

Dr. Fawn chuckled. "Well, at least it's festive."

Rudolph didn't find it amusing. He'd spent the morning dodging Dasher, who claimed Rudolph's glowing nose was "blinding his peripheral vision," and Comet, who insisted the brightness was interfering with his nap schedule. Even Prancer, who usually defended Rudolph, had suggested covering his nose with tinsel "for aesthetic reasons."

By lunchtime, Rudolph was ready to try anything to dim the glow. He trotted into the workshop, where Mrs. Claus was handing out her freshly baked cookies.

"Rudolph, dear, you don't look so good," she said, her brow furrowing.

"It's the flu," Rudolph said, sneezing mid-sentence. The resulting burst of light was bright enough to make a passing elf drop a tray of ornaments.

Mrs. Claus patted his shoulder sympathetically. "I've got just the thing for you. Wait right here."

A few minutes later, she returned with a steaming mug. "This is my special peppermint-ginger tea. It'll clear your sinuses and calm that glow in no time."

Rudolph eyed the mug sceptically but took a sip. His nose glowed brighter for a moment, then dimmed slightly. "It's... not bad," he admitted, though the ginger's spiciness made his eyes water.

Encouraged by the slight improvement, Rudolph decided to seek advice from the elves. Surely, with all their ingenuity, someone would have a solution.

Jingle, who was stationed at the sleigh maintenance desk, scratched his head thoughtfully. "Have you tried adjusting your diet? Maybe lay off the carrots for a while."

"Carrots? What's wrong with carrots?" Rudolph asked, bewildered.

"They're orange, right? Maybe they're fuelling the glow," Jingle said.

Rudolph rolled his eyes. "That's not how it works."

Sparkle, overhearing the conversation, chimed in. "What about a nose cozy? We could knit you something to cover it up!"

"A nose cozy?" Rudolph repeated, unimpressed.

"Yeah! Something cute with snowflakes on it!" Sparkle said excitedly.

Rudolph sighed. "Thanks, but I don't think I need my nose to look cute. I need it to stop glowing so much."

By evening, Rudolph had tried everything—Mrs. Claus's tea, an ice pack, even the bizarre "nose cozy" idea. Nothing worked. His glow remained as bright as ever, and his flu symptoms weren't helping. He lay down in his stable, exhausted and defeated, just as Santa strolled in to check on the reindeer.

"How's my favorite navigator?" Santa asked, crouching beside him.

"Not great," Rudolph admitted. "I feel awful, and everyone's making jokes about my glow."

Santa chuckled warmly. "Rudolph, your nose has always been more than just a light. It's a beacon of hope and joy. Even when you're under the weather, it reminds everyone of what Christmas is about—shining brightly, even in the darkest times."

"That's nice and all," Rudolph said, sniffling. "But it doesn't exactly help with the flu."

"Maybe not," Santa said, "but sometimes the best remedy is a little perspective. Besides, you'll be better in no time. We all rely on you, glow and all."

By the next morning, Rudolph's flu symptoms had begun to fade, and while his nose still glowed brightly, he felt a renewed sense of purpose. The reindeer and elves stopped teasing him and instead embraced his shining light as a symbol of the North Pole spirit.

As Rudolph trotted into the stables, Prancer nudged him playfully. "Feeling better, Glowbug?"

"Much better," Rudolph said, this time letting his nose shine proudly.

Because if there's one thing Rudolph had learned, it's that sometimes, even in flu season, a little light can make all the difference.

Chapter 5: Santa's Secret Hobby

The North Pole was a place of organized chaos in December. Santa's Workshop hummed with the clatter of toy assembly lines, the squeak of conveyor belts, and the constant chatter of elves hurrying to meet their deadlines. But amidst the frenzy, Santa Claus seemed unusually calm, even cheerful.

Unbeknownst to almost everyone at the North Pole, Santa had a secret—something he'd kept hidden for centuries. It wasn't scandalous or shocking; in fact, it was quite ordinary. Santa's secret was his hobby: wood carving.

For as long as he could remember, Santa had loved working with his hands. Long before he became the jolly icon of Christmas, he was a simple craftsman, making toys from scraps of wood. Over time, as his role grew into overseeing the entire operation, the demands of being "Santa Claus" left little room for his own creative pursuits.

But carving never left his heart.

It started small: an hour here, a stolen moment there. During breaks, while the elves bustled about or Mrs. Claus tested cookie recipes, Santa would slip away to a hidden workshop tucked behind the stables. No one paid much attention—after all, who would question Santa taking a moment to "check on the reindeer"?

Inside the workshop, the space was a stark contrast to the bustling toy factory. It was small and cozy, with a sturdy wooden table at its center, tools neatly organized along the walls, and shavings of pine and cedar scattered on the floor. The air was filled with the soothing scent of freshly carved wood.

Santa would settle into his chair, grab a block of wood, and let his hands do the work. He didn't need a plan or a blueprint; the shapes seemed to emerge naturally—tiny reindeer, delicate snowflakes, cheerful elves, and even an occasional snowman.

These figures weren't destined for the toy shop or anyone's stocking. They were just for him. Santa carved because it brought him peace—a quiet joy amid the whirlwind of holiday preparations.

One particularly hectic day in early December, the workshop was in chaos. An entire shipment of stuffed animals had been stitched with the wrong-coloured eyes, and an elf accidentally spilled glitter into the wrapping department, creating what could only be described as a sparkling snowstorm.

"Santa, we need you in the quality control department!" shouted Jingle, his voice barely audible over the din.

Santa nodded, hiding a sigh. He loved his work, truly, but sometimes the stress weighed heavily. "I'll be there in a moment," he said, giving Mrs. Claus a quick kiss on the cheek before slipping out the back door.

Instead of heading to quality control, Santa made a beeline for his hidden workshop. He closed the door behind him, took a deep breath, and grabbed a fresh block of pine.

"Let's see what you want to become," he murmured to the wood, smiling as he picked up his carving knife.

Time seemed to melt away as Santa worked. The rhythmic scrape of the knife against wood was meditative, and for the first time that day, he felt his shoulders relax. When he finally stepped back to examine his work, he'd carved a tiny replica of Dasher, complete with a proud stance and a slightly mischievous expression.

Santa chuckled. "Not bad, old boy," he said, placing the figure on a shelf already crowded with dozens of others.

Meanwhile, back in the main workshop, the elves were starting to notice Santa's frequent disappearances.

"Where does he go all the time?" Sparkle asked, balancing a pile of train wheels on her head.

"Probably taking a nap," Grizzle grumbled.

"Santa doesn't nap!" Sparkle said, horrified at the suggestion. "He's probably... I don't know, doing important Santa stuff."

"Like what? Writing poetry?" Grizzle snorted.

The mystery of Santa's whereabouts quickly became the talk of the workshop. Even Mrs. Claus noticed her husband's vanishing act, though she chose not to say anything. She knew Santa better than anyone and trusted he had his reasons.

The truth came out purely by accident.

One afternoon, Rudolph was wandering behind the stables, looking for a quiet spot to escape from Dasher's constant teasing. As he trotted along, he noticed a soft glow coming from a small window in the side of a building he'd never paid attention to before. Curious, he peeked inside.

What he saw left him stunned.

There was Santa, hunched over a workbench, carefully carving a tiny snowman. The figure was intricate, with tiny details etched into the hat and scarf. Rudolph couldn't believe his eyes. Santa wasn't checking a list or organizing the workshop; he was... playing with wood.

"Santa?" Rudolph said hesitantly, poking his head through the door.

Santa nearly jumped out of his chair, clutching the snowman like a child caught with his hand in the cookie jar.

"Rudolph! What are you doing here?"

"I could ask you the same thing," Rudolph replied, stepping inside. "What is this place?"

Santa hesitated, then sighed. "It's my workshop. My real workshop."

Rudolph blinked. "You mean... you do all this yourself?"

Santa nodded, setting the snowman on the table. "It's my hobby. My escape. Sometimes, when things get overwhelming, I come here to carve. It helps me focus and reminds me why I started doing this in the first place."

Rudolph looked around the room, his eyes wide. "You made all of these?"

"Yes," Santa said, a touch of pride in his voice. "It's not about making toys for others. These are just for me."

Word of Rudolph's discovery spread faster than a snowball rolling downhill. By the next morning, every elf in the workshop was whispering about Santa's secret.

"He carves wooden figures!" Sparkle said, barely able to contain her excitement.

"No way," Grizzle replied. "Santa doesn't have time for hobbies."

"Well, he does," Sparkle insisted. "And I think it's sweet."

The elves decided to see for themselves. Led by Rudolph, they crept to the hidden workshop late that afternoon, peeking inside one by one. Sure enough, there was Santa, happily carving a tiny elf figure.

The following morning, Santa walked into the main workshop, expecting the usual chaos. Instead, he was met with cheers and applause.

"What's all this about?" he asked, startled.

"We found your workshop!" Jingle shouted.

Santa froze. "You... what?"

Sparkle stepped forward, holding one of his wooden figures—a small, intricately carved sleigh. "We think it's amazing. You're not just Santa; you're an artist!"

Santa's cheeks turned redder than his coat. "I—well, thank you, but it's just a hobby. Nothing special."

"Are you kidding?" Grizzle said, holding up a carved reindeer. "These are incredible! You could sell them!"

Mrs. Claus stepped in, beaming with pride. "I knew you had a little secret, but I didn't realize how talented you are."

Santa smiled sheepishly. "It's not about the talent. It's about finding something that brings you peace. Something that reminds you why you love what you do."

The room fell silent for a moment as everyone took in his words. Then Sparkle grinned. "So... does this mean we can have one of your carvings for the workshop?"

Santa laughed. "We'll see."

From that day on, Santa's hobby was no longer a secret. His carvings became treasured decorations around the North Pole, reminding everyone that even the busiest, most magical people need a little time to themselves.

And Santa? He was happier than ever, knowing his little hobby had brought so much joy—not just to him, but to everyone around him.

Because sometimes, the smallest things can make the biggest difference.

Chapter 6: The Great Tinsel Debate

The North Pole workshop was usually a harmonious place, buzzing with the sound of toy assembly and the cheerful hum of carols. But one frosty December morning, the elves were anything but cheerful. The workshop had been thrown into utter chaos—not because of a toy shortage, a reindeer mishap, or a glitch in Santa's Naughty or Nice list.

No, this time, the culprit was tinsel.

It all started innocently enough. Sparkle the Elf had been tasked with decorating the central Christmas tree in the workshop—a towering evergreen that served as the centrepiece of holiday cheer. She had just finished stringing up the lights when Jingle strolled by, munching on a candy cane.

"Looking good," Jingle said, inspecting the tree. "But what tinsel are you going to use? Silver or gold?"

Sparkle froze. "Silver, of course. It's classic, elegant, timeless."

Jingle raised an eyebrow. "Silver? No way! Gold is way more festive. It's warm and bright—exactly what Christmas is about."

Sparkle spun around to face him, hands on her hips. "Excuse me? Silver tinsel reflects the lights better. Gold just looks gaudy."

"Gaudy?" Jingle gasped. "Gold is the traditional choice! If anything, silver is boring."

Within minutes, other elves began chiming in.

"She's right—silver is the best!" shouted Tinsel, an elf who was clearly biased given his name.

"No way, gold all the way!" yelled Grizzle, already stirring the pot.

By mid-morning, the workshop was split into two camps: Team Silver and Team Gold.

Team Silver, led by Sparkle, argued that silver was versatile, reflecting the tree's lights like tiny icicles. They even went as far as creating a chart showing how silver tinsel complemented all the workshop's other decorations, from the candy cane garlands to the glittering snowflakes hanging from the ceiling.

Team Gold, with Jingle at the helm, countered with their own arguments. Gold, they claimed, brought warmth to the tree and embodied the rich, glowing spirit of Christmas. They pointed out that Santa's sleigh was trimmed in gold, and even the star atop the tree was golden.

The debate escalated quickly.

"Silver looks like a bunch of icicles threw up on the tree!" Grizzle shouted.

"Oh yeah? Well, gold looks like melted coins dripped all over it!" Sparkle fired back.

By lunchtime, the argument had spilled into other parts of the workshop. Elves in the wrapping department started using only silver or gold ribbons, depending on their allegiance. Even the bakers were divided, with one group sprinkling silver sugar on cookies and the other dusting them with edible gold.

The tension was so thick you could cut it with a candy cane.

Meanwhile, Santa and Mrs. Claus were blissfully unaware of the brewing war. They were enjoying a quiet cup of cocoa in the kitchen when Jingle burst in.

"Santa, you've got to settle this!" he said, his face flushed with frustration.

"Settle what?" Santa asked, startled.

"The tinsel debate!" Jingle exclaimed. "Silver versus gold. It's tearing the workshop apart!"

Mrs. Claus exchanged a look with Santa and tried not to laugh. "You're serious?"

"Dead serious," Jingle said. "It's chaos in there!"

Santa sighed, setting down his mug. "I'll take a look."

When Santa entered the workshop, he was met with a scene of utter disarray. The elves were shouting at one another, waving strands of silver and gold tinsel like battle flags. The tree, which should have been a shining beacon of holiday cheer, stood half-decorated—its top half covered in silver and its bottom half draped in gold.

"Enough!" Santa's voice boomed, silencing the room. "What is going on here?"

Sparkle stepped forward, clutching a roll of silver tinsel. "Santa, we're trying to decide what tinsel to use on the tree. Silver is clearly the better choice."

"No, gold is better!" Jingle shouted from the other side of the room.

The elves immediately began shouting over each other again, and Santa raised his hands for quiet.

"Why does it have to be one or the other?" Santa asked.

The room fell silent.

"That's ridiculous," Grizzle said after a moment. "You can't mix silver and gold. It'll look like a mess."

"Actually," Santa said, stroking his beard, "I think it could be beautiful. Silver and gold complement each other, don't you think? Like snow on a golden sunrise."

Mrs. Claus, who had followed Santa into the workshop, nodded. "Santa's right. Christmas is about coming together. Why not let silver and gold share the spotlight?"

The elves exchanged hesitant glances.

To settle the matter, Santa proposed a challenge. "We'll split into two teams," he said. "One side will decorate half the tree in silver, and the other in gold. Then we'll mix the two styles at the end and see how it looks."

The elves reluctantly agreed, and soon the workshop was buzzing again. Sparkle and Jingle worked with their respective teams to create the most dazzling decorations they could imagine.

Team Silver added shimmering icicles, glittering snowflakes, and frosty ornaments. Team Gold countered with warm golden garlands, glowing candles, and bright star-shaped baubles.

Finally, the two teams came together to combine their efforts. Silver and gold tinsel were carefully intertwined, draping the tree in a harmonious blend of cool elegance and warm radiance.

When the tree was finished, the elves stepped back to admire their work. The result was breathtaking. The silver reflected the twinkling lights, while the gold added a warm glow that tied everything together.

"It's perfect," Sparkle admitted grudgingly.

"Yeah," Jingle said, crossing his arms. "I guess silver isn't so bad."

"And gold's not so gaudy after all," Sparkle replied with a smile.

Santa beamed. "Now that's the Christmas spirit! When we work together, the result is always better."

From that day on, the North Pole workshop adopted a new tradition: every tree would feature a mix of silver and gold decorations, symbolizing unity and cooperation. The elves even coined a new motto: "Silver and Gold—Better Together."

And every year, as Santa gazed at the beautifully decorated tree, he was reminded that even the smallest debates could lead to something truly magical.

Chapter 7: Elf Yoga Gone Wrong

At the North Pole, even elves needed to find ways to relax amidst the holiday chaos. For Sparkle the Elf, yoga was her sanctuary—a chance to unwind, find her inner peace, and escape the endless hum of the workshop's conveyor belts.

But it wasn't enough for Sparkle to practice yoga on her own. She believed in spreading the joy, which is why she'd started offering free yoga classes to her fellow elves.

The classes were small but growing in popularity. Every morning at 6 AM, Sparkle would roll out her peppermint-striped yoga mat in the workshop's breakroom, light a few cinnamon-scented candles, and lead her class through poses like "Candy Cane Twist" and "Gumdrop Warrior." It was serene, calming, and everything Sparkle loved.

Until the reindeer showed up.

It started innocently enough. Dasher had been trotting by the breakroom when he noticed Sparkle demonstrating a particularly elaborate pose to a group of elves.

"What are you doing?" he asked, poking his head through the door.

"It's called yoga," Sparkle replied, balancing on one foot in "Jingle Bell Tree" pose. "It helps with flexibility and relaxation. You should try it!"

Dasher snorted. "Reindeer don't need yoga. We're already flexible."

"Oh yeah?" Sparkle challenged. "Can you do this?"

She dropped into a perfect "Sugarplum Split," her arms raised gracefully above her head.

Dasher frowned. "That doesn't look so hard."

The next morning, Sparkle was midway through a class when the stable doors burst open. Dasher strolled in, followed by Prancer, Rudolph, and Comet.

"We're here for yoga," Dasher announced proudly.

Sparkle blinked. "Uh... are you sure?"

"Of course," Prancer said, stepping forward. "If it's good enough for the elves, it's good enough for us."

The elves exchanged nervous glances. Yoga was one thing, but reindeer yoga? That was uncharted territory.

"Well," Sparkle said, forcing a smile, "grab a mat and let's get started!"

From the very beginning, it was clear the reindeer were out of their element.

Sparkle began with a simple pose. "Let's start with 'Snowflake Stretch.' Just reach up as high as you can."

The elves followed her lead, arms stretching gracefully toward the ceiling. The reindeer, however, struggled. Dasher's antlers nearly knocked over one of Sparkle's candles, and Comet accidentally smacked Rudolph in the nose with his hoof.

"Watch it!" Rudolph grumbled, rubbing his glowing nose.

"Sorry," Comet said, clearly embarrassed.

Things only got worse as the class progressed.

"Next is 'Candy Cane Twist,'" Sparkle said, demonstrating the pose. "Just twist your body gently to the side and hold it there."

The elves managed it easily, but the reindeer were another story. Dasher got tangled in his own legs, Comet slipped on his mat, and Prancer ended up spinning in circles.

"Twist, don't twirl!" Sparkle called out, trying to suppress a laugh.

Meanwhile, Rudolph attempted the pose but overdid it, losing his balance and crashing into a stack of yoga mats.

By the time Sparkle introduced "Peppermint Plank," the reindeer were exhausted.

"This one's great for building core strength," Sparkle said. She dropped into a perfect plank, her body straight as an arrow.

The elves followed suit, holding the pose with determination. The reindeer, however, struggled to even get into position.

"Are you sure this is safe?" Prancer asked, his legs wobbling beneath him.

"Totally safe," Sparkle said, smiling.

Seconds later, Comet collapsed onto the mat with a loud thud. "I think I pulled something."

Dasher was shaking so hard his antlers rattled, and Prancer was sprawled out on the floor, groaning dramatically.

The real chaos began during "Reindeer Warrior Pose."

"This one's perfect for improving balance and strength," Sparkle said.

She demonstrated the pose: one leg extended behind her, arms stretched forward in a graceful arc. The elves copied her effortlessly.

The reindeer, on the other hand, were a disaster waiting to happen.

Dasher wobbled precariously, trying to lift one hoof off the ground. "How do you keep from falling over?"

"Practice!" Sparkle replied cheerfully.

Unfortunately, Dasher didn't have enough practice—or balance. He toppled sideways, crashing into Rudolph, who let out a startled yelp and accidentally knocked over Comet. The domino effect ended with Prancer colliding with a stack of chairs, sending them clattering to the ground.

The room erupted into chaos.

By the time Sparkle managed to restore order, the breakroom was a mess. Mats were scattered everywhere, chairs were overturned, and one of her candles had been snuffed out in the commotion.

"Okay," Sparkle said, clapping her hands. "Maybe we should skip to relaxation."

The reindeer eagerly agreed, flopping onto their mats in relief.

"Now, close your eyes and breathe deeply," Sparkle instructed. "Inhale... and exhale..."

For a few glorious moments, the room was silent. Sparkle finally felt a sense of calm returning.

Until Dasher started snoring.

"Seriously?" Prancer whispered, glaring at him.

"It's called relaxation," Dasher muttered, not even opening his eyes.

When the class finally ended, Sparkle stood at the door, watching the reindeer shuffle out with varying degrees of exhaustion and embarrassment.

"Thanks for letting us join," Rudolph said, his nose glowing faintly. "I think."

"Anytime," Sparkle said with a smile. "But maybe next time we'll stick to meditation."

Despite the chaos, Sparkle couldn't help but laugh as she cleaned up the breakroom. Sure, the class hadn't gone as planned, but it had been unforgettable.

And as she rolled up her peppermint-striped mat, she made a mental note: never underestimate the challenges of reindeer yoga.

Chapter 8: The Snowball Scandal

It started with a single snowball.

The wrapping department at Santa's Workshop was usually a peaceful place, filled with the soothing sounds of scissors snipping and paper crinkling. But on this particular day, the air was thick with tension. A new shipment of glittery wrapping paper had arrived, and the elves were not pleased.

"This stuff is impossible to work with," grumbled Grizzle, attempting to fold a corner. The glitter stuck to his hands, his face, and even his coffee mug. "It's like trying to wrap a gift in sandpaper."

"It's not so bad," Sparkle replied, tying a perfect bow on a freshly wrapped box. "You just need finesse."

Grizzle glared at her. "Finesse this," he muttered, crumpling up a handful of glitter paper and tossing it onto the floor.

From across the room, Jingle chuckled. "You know what you need, Grizzle? A little chill." He picked up a tiny snowball from a decorative display and lobbed it gently in Grizzle's direction.

It was meant as a joke, but the snowball hit Grizzle square in the forehead, leaving a streak of cold and a sprinkle of glitter behind.

The room went silent.

For a moment, Grizzle simply stared at Jingle, his face unreadable. Then, without a word, he reached into the display, grabbed his own snowball, and hurled it with surprising accuracy. It hit Jingle in the shoulder, sending a puff of snow and glitter into the air.

"Oh, it's on now!" Jingle shouted, grabbing another snowball.

What began as a harmless exchange quickly escalated. Sparkle ducked as a rogue snowball whizzed past her head, narrowly missing a stack of perfectly wrapped gifts.

"Hey!" she shouted. "Take it outside!"

But no one was listening.

Within minutes, the wrapping department had transformed into a war zone. Elves were diving behind tables, using rolls of wrapping paper as shields. Snowballs flew through the air, leaving trails of glitter wherever they landed.

Tinsel, the department supervisor, burst in, waving her clipboard. "What is going on here?"

A snowball hit her square in the chest, sending her clipboard clattering to the floor.

"Oh, that's it," Tinsel growled, grabbing a handful of snow. "If you can't beat 'em, join 'em!"

Chaos erupted as more elves joined the fray. Sparkle tried to maintain order, but it was no use. Someone had upturned a box of decorative snow, and now the entire department was blanketed in white fluff.

Grizzle and Jingle had taken cover behind a tower of wrapped presents, lobbing snowballs with military precision. "Take that!" Grizzle shouted, sending a snowball directly into Tinsel's perfectly braided hair.

"You'll pay for that!" Tinsel yelled, launching a glitter-filled snowball in retaliation.

Meanwhile, Sparkle found herself caught in the crossfire. She crouched behind a table, clutching a roll of wrapping paper like a lifeline. "This is insane," she muttered, dodging yet another snowball.

The sound of jingling bells silenced the room.

Everyone froze as Santa Claus himself appeared in the doorway, his eyes wide with surprise. Behind him stood Mrs. Claus, holding a tray of cookies.

"What is going on here?" Santa boomed, his voice echoing through the snowy battlefield.

The elves scrambled to their feet, brushing glitter and fake snow from their clothes. Grizzle tried to hide a snowball behind his back, but it melted in his hands, leaving a soggy mess.

"Uh… team-building exercise?" Jingle offered weakly.

Santa raised an eyebrow.

Mrs. Claus, ever the peacemaker, stepped forward. "Well, it certainly looks like everyone's having fun," she said with a smile. "But perhaps it's time to clean up?"

Under Santa's watchful gaze, the elves set to work restoring order. Wrapping paper was restocked, ribbons were untangled, and the floor was swept clean of snow and glitter.

"I don't want to see another snowball in this department," Santa said sternly, though there was a twinkle in his eye. "Is that clear?"

"Yes, Santa," the elves mumbled in unison.

As Santa and Mrs. Claus left the room, Grizzle leaned over to Jingle. "Totally worth it," he whispered.

By the end of the day, the wrapping department was back to its usual state of organized chaos. The snowball fight was already becoming the stuff of legend, with elves swapping stories about their best throws and close calls.

And though no one would dare admit it, a secret stash of snowballs remained hidden in the breakroom freezer—just in case.

Because at the North Pole, even the most well-behaved elves couldn't resist a little mischief now and then.

Chapter 9: The Naughty List Dilemma

Santa Claus sat at his desk in the quiet of his study, the soft glow of the fireplace casting long shadows across the room. Before him was the Naughty List—a meticulously compiled record of every child who'd misbehaved during the year. It wasn't a list Santa enjoyed maintaining. In fact, it was his least favorite part of the job. But Christmas magic had its rules, and part of that magic was ensuring the Naughty and Nice Lists were fair.

This year, however, one name was giving him more trouble than usual: Emily Carter, age eight.

Emily had been added to the Naughty List in June after what could only be described as an epic temper tantrum at the neighbourhood park. The tantrum had escalated to the point where she'd not only knocked over her best friend's ice cream cone but also pushed her little brother into a muddy puddle. Witnesses (namely two elves on assignment) had reported it as a clear case of Naughty List behaviour.

Since then, Emily's name had remained on the list, with further reports of minor squabbles and occasional bouts of sass. Santa had tried not to think too much about it—after all, kids made mistakes, and the system was designed to give them time to learn and improve.

But last night, something unexpected had arrived: a handwritten letter from Emily.

Santa carefully unfolded the letter again, the neat, slightly wobbly handwriting tugging at his heartstrings.

Dear Santa,

I know I haven't been very good this year. I was mean to my brother, and I said some things I shouldn't have. I'm really sorry. I've been trying to be better—I even let my brother have the last cookie yesterday. I hope you'll forgive me. I promise I'll do better next year.

Love,
Emily

P.S. If you can still come to my house, I'd really love a puppy.

Santa sighed, running a hand through his snowy beard. The rules were clear: once a child was on the Naughty List, they had to demonstrate consistent good behaviour to earn their way off. An apology letter alone wasn't enough.

And yet...

Santa glanced at the report from his monitoring elves. Emily had been trying. There was evidence of her sharing toys, helping her mother with chores, and even apologizing to her friend for the ice cream incident. But there were also slip-ups: an argument over a board game, a minor tantrum about bedtime, and an unkind comment to her brother just last week.

"Not exactly Nice List material," Santa muttered, though his heart ached to admit it.

Mrs. Claus entered the study, holding a steaming mug of cocoa. "Still agonizing over the list?" she asked, placing the mug on his desk.

Santa nodded. "It's Emily Carter. She sent an apology letter."

Mrs. Claus leaned over to read the letter. When she was done, she smiled gently. "Sounds like she's trying."

"She is," Santa admitted. "But is it enough? If I take her off the Naughty List, it wouldn't be fair to the other children who worked hard all year to stay on the Nice List."

Mrs. Claus sat down across from him. "And if you don't, what message does that send? That there's no point in trying to be better?"

Santa pondered her words as he sipped his cocoa. The Naughty List wasn't meant to be a punishment; it was meant to teach. But where was the line between fairness and forgiveness?

He turned to his Big Book of Christmas Guidelines, flipping through the pages until he found the section on the Naughty List. The rules were strict but not absolute. A child could be removed from the list under "exceptional circumstances," though the guidelines left it up to Santa's discretion.

Exceptional circumstances. Santa stared at the phrase, tapping his pen on the desk.

"Maybe I should check in on her," Santa said suddenly.

Mrs. Claus raised an eyebrow. "You mean spy on her?"

"Not spy," Santa said defensively. "Observe. A quick visit won't hurt."

Mrs. Claus chuckled. "Do what you need to, dear. But remember, Christmas is about more than just rules. It's about hope and second chances."

That night, Santa donned his coat and boots and headed to the North Pole's observation station. The elves there had access to the magic snow globe, a tool that allowed Santa to see any child in the world.

"Emily Carter, please," Santa said, leaning over the globe.

The swirling mist cleared to reveal Emily's living room. She was sitting cross-legged on the floor, carefully wrapping a gift. Her younger brother, Max, sat beside her, holding a roll of tape.

"What are you doing?" Max asked.

"It's for Mom," Emily said, tying a slightly crooked bow around the package. "I saved up my allowance to buy her a scarf."

Max looked at her with wide eyes. "You spent all your money on that?"

Emily shrugged. "She's always cold, and she doesn't buy nice things for herself."

Santa watched as Emily handed the gift to Max. "Here, you can give it to her from both of us."

Max grinned. "Thanks, Emily!"

Santa's heart swelled. He closed the snow globe, a smile tugging at his lips.

Back in his study, Santa picked up his pen and hovered it over Emily's name. He hesitated, then flipped to the page for the Nice List. Slowly, deliberately, he added her name.

On Christmas morning, Emily woke to find a small box under the tree with her name on it. Inside was a note in flowing script:

Dear Emily,

Thank you for your letter and for trying to be better. Remember, it's not about being perfect, it's about learning and growing. Keep being kind to others, and you'll find the magic of Christmas grows with you.

Merry Christmas,

Santa

Beneath the note was a small stuffed puppy with a tag that read: "Practice pet care for the real thing!"

Emily hugged the toy to her chest, her heart filled with joy.

At the North Pole, Santa leaned back in his chair, feeling lighter than he had in days. The Naughty List had its place, but so did forgiveness.

After all, Christmas wasn't just about who made the Nice List. It was about spreading love, learning from mistakes, and believing in the possibility of a brighter tomorrow.

Chapter 10: The Chimney Tester's Journal

Entry 1: The Most Overlooked Job at the North Pole

They call me Flicker the Chimney Tester, though around the workshop, most just call me "that unlucky elf." Chimney testing isn't exactly the most glamorous job, but someone's got to do it. After all, if Santa can't fit down a chimney on Christmas Eve, the whole operation is at risk.

The job is simple in theory: measure the chimney, check the soot levels, and make sure it's safe for Santa's grand descent. Simple, right? Wrong. Chimneys are tiny, dirty, and filled with surprises no elf should have to encounter.

Take today, for example.

Entry 2: When Chimneys Fight Back

My first stop this morning was a cozy little house on Maple Lane. The chimney looked promising—wide enough, not too tall, and freshly swept. I climbed to the roof, trusty tape measure in hand, and lowered myself into the chimney.

Things were going fine until I reached halfway down. That's when I felt it: a tickle on my leg.

At first, I thought it was soot. Then it moved.

It was a squirrel.

Before I could react, the little guy panicked, running up my leg and over my head, leaving claw marks in his wake. I let out a very un-elflike scream and scrambled out of the chimney so fast I nearly slid off the roof.

Entry 3: What Goes Down Must Come Up

After surviving the squirrel incident, I headed to my second house. This chimney was much narrower, and as soon as I started climbing down, I realized I might have overestimated my own flexibility.

Halfway down, I got stuck.

"Stay calm, Flicker," I told myself, trying to wiggle free. But the more I wiggled, the more wedged I became. I reached for my radio to call for backup, only to realize I'd left it on the roof.

After about ten minutes of frantic struggling, gravity finally took over. I popped free and landed in the fireplace below—right into a pile of soot. The family cat, lounging nearby, took one look at me and hissed before darting out of the room.

At least I know the chimney works.

Entry 4: The Haunted Chimney

Not all chimneys are created equal. Some are simple and straightforward, while others seem to have been designed by mad architects.

House #3 fell into the latter category. The chimney twisted and turned like a corkscrew, with sharp angles that made climbing nearly impossible. But the real problem wasn't the design—it was the noise.

About halfway down, I started hearing whispers.

"Hello?" I called, my voice echoing off the bricks.

No response.

I continued my descent, but the whispers grew louder. "Flicker," they seemed to say.

At this point, I was convinced the chimney was haunted. I climbed back to the roof as fast as I could, only to discover the source of the whispers: two kids, hiding in the attic, using a walkie-talkie to scare me.

Santa better bring them coal.

Entry 5: The Marshmallow Incident

By midday, I was exhausted but determined to finish my route. House #4 had a short, squat chimney that looked like a piece of cake compared to the others. I dropped in, checked the width, and was about to climb out when I smelled something strange.

Marshmallows.

Curious, I leaned closer to the fireplace and discovered a half-melted s'more stuck to the bricks. Before I could move away, the gooey mess caught on my sleeve, pulling me forward.

Long story short, I spent the next ten minutes trying to scrape melted marshmallow out of my hair. Lesson learned: never underestimate the hazards of late-night snacking.

Entry 6: The Great Chimney Debate

House #5 wasn't particularly memorable for the chimney itself—it was the homeowners who made it interesting.

I'd just finished my inspection and was climbing out when I overheard the family arguing.

"We don't even use the chimney!" the dad said.

"Well, what if Santa needs it?" the mom replied.

"I thought he used the front door!"

I couldn't help myself. I poked my soot-covered head out of the fireplace and said, "Santa prefers chimneys, but he'll make do."

The family screamed, the dad fell off the couch, and I decided it was time to make a quick exit.

Entry 7: When It's All Worth It

My final stop of the day was a little cottage on the edge of town. The chimney was old and crumbling, and I was worried it wouldn't pass inspection. As I worked, I noticed a little girl peeking at me through the window.

"Are you one of Santa's elves?" she asked when I climbed down.

I nodded, brushing soot off my hat. "I sure am."

Her face lit up. "Can you tell Santa I've been extra good this year?"

"Of course," I said, smiling.

As I walked back to my sleigh, I realized that, for all the mishaps, this job isn't so bad after all.

Entry 8: Back at the Workshop

When I returned to the North Pole, the other elves were waiting for my report.

"How'd it go?" Jingle asked, smirking.

I handed him my soot-streaked clipboard. "Let's just say Santa owes me a bonus."

That night, as I scrubbed marshmallow out of my hair, I couldn't help but laugh. Being a chimney tester might not be glamorous, but it sure is memorable.

And hey, if Santa gets stuck this Christmas, it won't be because of me.

Chapter 11: The Candy Cane Conundrum

Pepper the elf was having a typical morning in the candy department of Santa's Workshop. The machines hummed as they churned out a steady stream of peppermint candy canes, their red and white stripes swirling in perfect harmony. As the lead operator of the Peppermint Production Line, Pepper took immense pride in her work.

But as she sipped her cocoa and checked her clipboard, something unusual caught her eye.

"Wait a second..." she muttered, flipping through her inventory sheet. The numbers didn't add up.

According to the production log, the factory had already surpassed its annual candy cane quota—by 10,000 canes.

Pepper's heart sank. Candy canes were one of Santa's most beloved treats, but there was only so much demand for them. If Santa found out she'd overshot the target by such a large margin, it would be a disaster.

"How did this happen?" she muttered, pacing back and forth. "The machines must've been running double shifts without me realizing it!"

Pepper knew she had to act fast. If she could quietly deal with the surplus before anyone noticed, she might avoid a lecture from the Head Elf—and worse, Santa's disappointed frown.

Her first thought was to distribute the extra candy canes around the workshop.

She loaded a crate onto a sleigh and zoomed to the reindeer stables. "Hey, Dasher!" she called, holding up a candy cane. "Want a treat?"

Dasher sniffed the candy cane suspiciously. "Peppermint? I prefer carrots."

Pepper frowned. "What about you, Rudolph?"

Rudolph shook his head. "It makes my nose glow even brighter. Not ideal for stealthy landings."

Dejected, Pepper left the stables and tried her luck in the wrapping department.

"Free candy canes!" she announced, placing a box on the counter.

Jingle, who was busy tying bows, glanced up. "Pepper, we're already drowning in candy canes. Have you seen the breakroom? It's like a peppermint explosion in there."

Next, Pepper tried to stash the extras in the breakroom itself. She shoved boxes of candy canes under the table, behind the cocoa machine, and even inside the cupboard labelled "Elf Snacks."

"Out of sight, out of mind," she whispered, dusting off her hands.

But her plan quickly backfired.

"Who put candy canes in the cocoa machine?" Sparkle yelled later that afternoon, holding up a sticky mess of red and white goo.

Pepper ducked behind a shelf, her cheeks flushing redder than a candy cane stripe.

Desperate, she considered dumping the surplus outside. Under the cover of night, she loaded another sleigh with crates and flew to the edge of the North Pole.

"This should do it," she said, preparing to toss the candy canes into a snowbank.

But just as she was about to heave the first crate, she heard a deep voice behind her.

"Pepper."

She froze, turning slowly to see Santa standing there, his hands on his hips.

"Care to explain?" he asked, raising an eyebrow.

Pepper's ears drooped. "It's the candy canes, Santa. I accidentally made too many, and I didn't know what to do. I didn't want to bother you with it, so I tried to fix it myself."

Santa stroked his beard thoughtfully. "You know, Pepper, honesty is always the best policy. But instead of hiding the problem, why don't we find a creative solution?"

Pepper blinked. "A solution? Like what?"

The next morning, Santa gathered the elves for an announcement.

"This year, we're starting a new tradition," he said, holding up one of the surplus candy canes. "These extra candy canes will be used to spread Christmas cheer beyond our usual deliveries. We'll distribute them to hospitals, community centres, and even the Yeti village in the mountains!"

The elves cheered, and Pepper felt a wave of relief.

Over the next few days, the workshop buzzed with excitement as elves packed the extra candy canes into colorful boxes for their new recipients. Even Rudolph helped out, though he insisted on wearing sunglasses to avoid nose-glow embarrassment.

When the last box was loaded onto Santa's sleigh, Pepper finally relaxed.

"Thank you, Santa," she said. "I thought I'd ruined Christmas, but you turned it into something even better."

Santa chuckled. "Christmas isn't about perfection, Pepper. It's about making the most of what we have—and spreading joy wherever we can."

As Santa flew off that night, delivering the surplus candy canes to unexpected places, Pepper watched the sleigh disappear into the sky.

She made a mental note to double-check her production quotas next year—but for now, she was just grateful for a holiday saved by teamwork and a little Christmas magic.

Chapter 12: Dasher's Diva Moment

With Christmas Eve only a few days away, the reindeer training sessions were in full swing. The snow-covered runway outside Santa's Workshop echoed with the sound of hooves pounding against the packed snow and the occasional encouraging shout from Rudolph, who had been promoted to lead trainer this year.

Everything was going according to plan—until Dasher, the fleet-footed veteran of Santa's sleigh team, decided it was time for a break.

"I'm not running another lap until I get a hooficure," Dasher announced, coming to a dramatic halt in the middle of the runway.

The other reindeer skidded to a stop, their breath fogging the frosty air.

"Seriously, Dasher?" Prancer said, rolling his eyes. "We're on a tight schedule!"

"Your hooves look fine to me," said Comet, glancing down.

Dasher sniffed indignantly. "Fine? Fine is not good enough for Christmas Eve. Do you know how many people will be watching us? Photos, videos, drones. I refuse to pull the sleigh with unpolished hooves!"

Rudolph trotted over, his nose glowing faintly in the dim light. "Dasher, come on. We've got work to do. You can get a hooficure after the big night."

Dasher shook his head, his antlers gleaming in the moonlight. "No can do. My hooves are chipped, uneven, and completely unacceptable. It's hooficure or bust."

Rudolph sighed. "Okay, fine. Five minutes. But after that, we're back on the runway."

Dasher smirked. "Five minutes? Oh, sweetie, you don't know how hooficures work."

Inside the reindeer stables, Dasher settled onto a cushioned stool while Sparkle the elf, who had reluctantly agreed to assist, rummaged through a kit of hoof polish and buffers.

"This is ridiculous," Sparkle muttered, holding up a bottle of glittery gold polish. "You're delaying the entire training session for shiny hooves?"

"Not just shiny," Dasher corrected. "Radiant. I'm thinking a gold finish with snowflake accents. Something subtle but festive."

"Subtle?" Sparkle repeated, eyeing the glitter. "Right."

Meanwhile, back on the runway, the other reindeer were growing restless.

"This is throwing off our rhythm," Blitzen grumbled, stomping a hoof. "We've got a new landing pattern to perfect, and Dasher's getting his hooves done?"

"We should just train without him," Cupid suggested.

"We can't," Rudolph said, pacing. "Dasher's our fastest runner. Without him, the formations don't work."

"Then maybe we need to remind him what's at stake," Prancer said with a mischievous glint in his eye.

By the time Dasher returned to the runway, his hooves gleaming like freshly polished ornaments, the other reindeer were lined up, their expressions a mix of exasperation and amusement.

"There he is," Prancer said, his voice dripping with sarcasm. "The star of the show."

Dasher ignored him, holding up a hoof for inspection. "Sparkle really outdid herself, didn't she? I mean, look at this shine!"

"You've got your hooficure," Rudolph said firmly. "Now let's get back to work."

Dasher sauntered into position, his hooves clicking on the icy runway. "Fine, but don't blame me if everyone's staring at my feet on Christmas Eve."

Training resumed, but it wasn't long before Dasher's diva moment came back to haunt him. As the team practiced a particularly tricky midair pivot, Dasher's freshly polished hooves slipped on the sleigh's icy platform.

"Whoa!" he shouted, skidding into Blitzen and knocking him off balance.

The sleigh tilted dangerously to one side, sending a pile of gift boxes tumbling into the snow below.

"Dasher!" Rudolph yelled, flying over to steady the sleigh. "What happened?"

"It's the polish!" Dasher admitted, his cheeks turning red. "It's too slippery!"

After a round of grumbling and a few well-placed "I told you so's," the team took an extended break while Sparkle worked on buffing Dasher's hooves back to their natural state.

As she finished, she smirked at him. "Radiant enough for you?"

Dasher sighed. "Okay, maybe I overdid it. But you've got to admit, they looked incredible."

By the end of the day, the team was back on track, and Dasher had learned an important lesson about priorities.

As they trotted back to the stables, Prancer nudged him. "So, do we have time for my antler wax appointment tomorrow?"

The entire team burst out laughing, even Dasher.

"Very funny," he said, rolling his eyes. "But seriously, have you seen my antlers? They could use a touch-up."

And with that, the reindeer team was ready for Christmas Eve—hooves, antlers, and all.

Chapter 13: Mrs. Claus's Bake-Off Drama

Every year at the North Pole, the elves eagerly anticipated one event almost as much as Christmas itself: the Annual Elf Bake-Off. It was a chance for elves from every department—whether they worked in toy assembly, candy production, or sleigh maintenance—to show off their culinary skills and earn the coveted title of "Master Baker of the North Pole."

As always, Mrs. Claus was the esteemed judge of the competition. Known for her expertise in holiday treats, she was the undisputed queen of cookies, cakes, and pies.

This year, however, her judgment would be put to the ultimate test.

The workshop buzzed with excitement as the elves filed into the grand kitchen, carrying trays of their best confections. The room was decked out in peppermint-striped banners, glittering fairy lights, and a long table covered in red velvet, ready to display the baked masterpieces.

"Welcome, everyone!" Mrs. Claus announced, standing at the head of the room. Her apron bore the words "Official Taste Tester" in bold, embroidered letters. "I'm thrilled to be judging this year's competition. As always, the winner will receive the Golden Whisk and bragging rights for the whole year!"

The elves cheered, their eyes sparkling with determination.

As the competition began, Mrs. Claus moved down the table, tasting each entry and jotting down notes.

First up was Jingle's Triple Chocolate Fudge Cake. It was rich, decadent, and topped with a chocolate sleigh pulled by sugar reindeer.

"Delightful," Mrs. Claus said, scribbling on her clipboard.

Next came Sparkle's Candy Cane Macarons, perfectly round and striped in red and white.

"So festive!" Mrs. Claus exclaimed.

Then there was Tinsel's Gingerbread House Extravaganza, complete with icing icicles and marshmallow snowmen.

"Incredible attention to detail," Mrs. Claus noted, licking a stray dollop of frosting from her finger.

But the most controversial entry came from Grizzle, the famously grumpy elf. Grizzle was not known for his culinary skills—in fact, most elves avoided anything he baked. But this year, he had shocked everyone by entering a towering Holiday Fruitcake.

"I made it dense," Grizzle said proudly as Mrs. Claus approached. "Really dense."

Mrs. Claus hesitated before cutting a slice. Sure enough, her knife barely made it through the solid cake. But when she took a bite, she was surprised.

"Well," she said, struggling to chew, "it's... hearty."

After tasting all the entries, Mrs. Claus retreated to her judging chair to tally up the scores. The elves waited anxiously, some pacing, others nibbling nervously on leftover crumbs.

When Mrs. Claus finally stood to announce the winner, the room fell silent.

"This year's winner," she began, "is... Grizzle's Holiday Fruitcake!"

The room erupted—partly in cheers, partly in gasps.

"Grizzle?!" Sparkle whispered to Jingle, wide-eyed. "He won?"

Grizzle, for his part, looked as shocked as anyone. "I... I did it?"

Mrs. Claus handed him the Golden Whisk, beaming. "Congratulations, Grizzle! Your fruitcake was truly one-of-a-kind."

But as the elves crowded around to congratulate Grizzle, Mrs. Claus glanced at her clipboard and froze.

"Oh no," she whispered, realizing her mistake. In her excitement (and perhaps after too much sugar), she had misread her notes. Grizzle's fruitcake hadn't earned the highest score—it was actually Sparkle's Candy Cane Macarons.

Mrs. Claus's heart sank. What was she supposed to do? Publicly rescind Grizzle's win and risk humiliating him? Or let the mistake stand and deny Sparkle her rightful prize?

By the time the bake-off ended, Mrs. Claus still hadn't corrected the error. Grizzle was holding his whisk aloft like a trophy, while Sparkle clapped politely, though her smile didn't quite reach her eyes.

That night, Mrs. Claus confided in Santa.

"I feel terrible," she said, pacing in the kitchen. "Sparkle deserves that whisk, but I don't want to hurt Grizzle's feelings. He's so proud of himself."

Santa stroked his beard thoughtfully. "What if we found a way to make it right without taking anything away from Grizzle?"

The next morning, Mrs. Claus called a meeting in the workshop.

"I've been thinking about yesterday's bake-off," she said, addressing the elves. "While Grizzle's fruitcake was an incredible feat, Sparkle's Candy Cane Macarons were equally spectacular. So, I've decided to award a special prize this year—Sparkle, you'll receive the Silver Spatula for Most Festive Creation!"

The elves cheered, and Sparkle's face lit up.

As she accepted her prize, she said, "Thank you, Mrs. Claus. I'm just happy everyone enjoyed my macarons."

Grizzle approached Sparkle afterward, holding his Golden Whisk.

"Hey," he said gruffly, "I know my fruitcake wasn't actually better than your macarons. I'm not much of a baker, but it felt good to win something for once."

Sparkle smiled. "Your fruitcake was... unforgettable, Grizzle. And besides, we both won something. That's what Christmas is about, right? Sharing the joy."

Grizzle nodded. "Thanks, Sparkle. Maybe next year I'll make something edible."

In the end, the bake-off was remembered as one of the most heartwarming in North Pole history. And while Mrs. Claus vowed to double-check her notes next year, she couldn't help but smile.

After all, a little Christmas spirit—and a lot of sugar—had turned a potential disaster into a celebration of kindness and camaraderie.

Chapter 14: The Wrapping Paper Wrangle

The wrapping department was supposed to be the most organized part of Santa's Workshop. With its neatly stacked rolls of paper, color-coded ribbons, and perfectly symmetrical bows, it was a place of precision and pride. But when the shipment of glittery wrapping paper arrived that morning, all that precision went right out the window.

It started with an innocent mistake. Tinsel the elf, who oversaw inventory, hadn't realized the wrapping paper supplier had switched to an ultra-glitter formula—a "new and improved" version designed to sparkle brighter and stick to everything.

When the first roll was unwrapped, Sparkle, the department's fastest gift wrapper, paused mid-ribbon curl. "Uh, Tinsel? Did you notice the glitter?"

Tinsel glanced over, frowning. "What glitter?"

Sparkle held up the shimmering paper, her hands already coated in a fine layer of gold sparkles.

"Oh no," Tinsel groaned, realizing the extent of the problem. "It's everywhere, isn't it?"

Within minutes, the glitter began spreading like wildfire. It clung to the elves' hands, faces, and clothing. It coated the conveyor belts, the scissors, even the cocoa mugs in the breakroom.

"This stuff is a menace!" Grizzle shouted, shaking a roll of paper and creating a cloud of glitter that settled on Jingle's head.

"Hey!" Jingle yelled, brushing glitter from his hair. "I look like a disco ball!"

"Maybe it's festive," Sparkle suggested, trying to see the bright side as she wiped glitter from her nose.

"Festive? This stuff is worse than snowball fights in the breakroom," Grizzle snapped, gesturing to the floor, which now sparkled as if it were paved with gold.

As the elves scrambled to contain the mess, more rolls of glittery paper were unwrapped, making the situation exponentially worse. The conveyor belt jammed when glitter clogged the gears, sending half-wrapped presents tumbling to the floor.

"It's in my ears," Tinsel groaned, trying to shake glitter out of her hair.

"And my cocoa!" Sparkle added, holding up her mug, which now glimmered with golden specks.

"Forget the cocoa," Grizzle said. "It's in my sandwich!"

Meanwhile, back in the main workshop, Santa and Mrs. Claus were conducting a sleigh inspection when a frazzled Jingle burst in.

"Santa! Mrs. Claus! We have a situation in the wrapping department."

Santa raised an eyebrow. "What kind of situation?"

Jingle hesitated. "The glittery kind."

When Santa arrived at the wrapping department, he couldn't believe his eyes.

Elves were slipping on glitter-coated floors, half-wrapped gifts were piled in disarray, and a thick layer of sparkle hung in the air like a golden fog. Even the candy cane garlands on the walls were glimmering unnaturally.

"What happened here?" Santa asked, his voice booming.

"Glitter wrapping paper," Tinsel said miserably, holding up a roll as evidence. A cascade of glitter fell from it, landing on Santa's boots.

Mrs. Claus stifled a laugh. "Well, it certainly looks... festive."

Santa cleared his throat. "All right, team. Let's clean up this mess and get back on track. We can't let glitter slow us down!"

The elves rallied, armed with brooms, dusters, and—much to everyone's amusement—a vacuum named Vinnie that Sparkle brought in from the breakroom.

"Let's do this!" Sparkle shouted, firing up Vinnie and sucking up a swirling pile of glitter.

It took hours of hard work, but by evening, the wrapping department was back in order—mostly. The elves were still sparkling like stars, and the conveyor belt gave off the occasional glitter puff, but the gifts were wrapped, and the chaos had been contained.

Santa inspected the finished presents and smiled. "They may be a bit shinier than usual, but they look beautiful."

"Let's hope the kids like glitter," Sparkle said with a grin, wiping her hands on her already glitter-covered apron.

As the elves finally sat down to rest, Mrs. Claus handed out mugs of cocoa. "Next time," she said, raising her mug, "we'll double-check the wrapping paper order. But for now, let's toast to teamwork—and maybe avoid glitter for a while."

The elves laughed and clinked their mugs, their spirits as bright as the glitter-covered workshop around them.

Because even in the chaos of the Wrapping Paper Wrangle, they'd managed to keep the Christmas magic alive.

Chapter 15: An Elf's Christmas Crush

December 15th

Dear Diary,

I never thought I'd be one of those elves. You know, the kind who gets tongue-tied and blush every time someone says "hello." But here I am, Jingle the Elf, acting like a total snowflake whenever they walk into the room.

I'm talking about Sparkle.

Sparkle, with the perfect ribbon curls in her hair, the kind of laugh that makes tinsel feel dull, and the way she can tie the most flawless bow you've ever seen in under three seconds. Is it weird to fall for someone over their ribbon-tying skills? Asking for a friend.

December 16th

Dear Diary,

Today was a disaster. Sparkle came by the toy assembly line to borrow some scissors, and I panicked. Instead of saying, "Here you go," like a normal elf, I said, "Happy scissors!"

HAPPY SCISSORS.

What does that even mean? She just smiled and said, "Thanks, Jingle," like I didn't just invent the worst catchphrase in elf history.

Later, Grizzle caught me staring at Sparkle while she wrapped presents. He smirked and said, "Got your eye on Sparkle, huh?" I denied it, of course, but he just laughed. "Good luck," he said. "She's way out of your league."

Gee, thanks for the encouragement, Grizzle.

December 17th

Dear Diary,

I think Sparkle likes candy canes. I saw her nibbling on one during break today. So naturally, I grabbed a handful from the breakroom and left them on her workstation with a little note that said, "Sweet for someone sweet."

Was it too much? Too little? Too cryptic? I spent the rest of the day avoiding her, convinced she'd figure out it was me and think I was weird.

Then, right before the end of the shift, I saw her tucking one of the candy canes into her pocket with a smile.

Am I overthinking this? Probably. But what if I'm not?

December 18th

Dear Diary,

We worked together today on the big Christmas tree display. I was in charge of hanging ornaments, and Sparkle was handling the bows. At one point, we reached for the same branch, and our hands touched.

I swear, it was like fireworks went off in my head. I stammered something about how "branches are tricky," and Sparkle just laughed.

"Branches are tricky?" she said. "Good one, Jingle."

I can't tell if she was teasing me or being nice. Either way, her laugh made my ears turn redder than Santa's suit.

December 19th

Dear Diary,

I overheard Sparkle talking to Tinsel today. She was saying how she wishes she had a little more "holiday magic" in her life. "Not the kind we make in the workshop," she said, "but the kind that feels special, you know?"

Does that mean she's looking for someone? Could that someone be me? Or am I just reading too much into this?

Either way, I decided to leave another note. This one said, "Sometimes the best magic is closer than you think." I didn't sign it. Let's see if she figures it out.

December 20th

Dear Diary,

Sparkle found the note. She was holding it when she walked into the wrapping department, looking around like she was searching for someone. For a split second, I thought she was about to ask if it was me.

Then Grizzle popped in and said, "What's that?" Sparkle tucked the note away and said, "Oh, just something sweet someone left for me."

Someone sweet. That's a good sign, right?

December 21st

Dear Diary,

Today, Mrs. Claus asked Sparkle to help her with the cookie decorations, and I somehow managed to end up in the kitchen, too. We spent the afternoon icing sugar cookies and sneaking tastes of frosting.

At one point, Sparkle got a little frosting on her nose, and I said, "Looks like you're the sweetest cookie here."

She laughed and said, "You're such a dork, Jingle."

A dork! She called me a dork! That's practically flirting, right?

December 22nd

Dear Diary,

I think I've got to tell her.

Christmas is only a few days away, and if I don't say something now, I'll regret it all year. But how do I tell Sparkle how I feel without making it awkward? Do I just blurt it out? Write another note? Bake her a cookie shaped like a heart?

I asked Tinsel for advice, and she said, "Just be honest. Sparkle likes honest elves."

Easier said than done, Tinsel.

December 23rd

Dear Diary,

I did it. I told Sparkle.

We were in the breakroom, decorating the little tree we keep there for the elves. I handed her an ornament I'd carved—a tiny candy cane with her name on it.

She looked at it and smiled. "This is so sweet! Did you make this for me?"

I nodded, my palms sweating. "I, uh, wanted to give you something special. Because you're... well... special."

Her cheeks turned pink. "That's really kind of you, Jingle."

I think I blacked out after that because the next thing I remember, she was hugging me.

December 24th

Dear Diary,

Best. Christmas. Ever.

Sparkle and I worked side by side on Santa's sleigh prep, and she kept the candy cane ornament in her pocket the whole time. When Santa took off, she grabbed my hand and said, "Thanks for making this season magical, Jingle."

Maybe next year, I'll be brave enough to call her my girlfriend. But for now, I'm just happy knowing I made her smile.

Christmas magic isn't just for kids—it's for elves, too.

Chapter 16: The Gift Mix-Up Meltdown

The North Pole workshop had never been busier. With Christmas Eve just hours away, the elves worked frantically to load Santa's sleigh. Ribbons were tied, bows were fluffed, and the air was filled with the sound of cheerful carols and the occasional jingle of reindeer bells.

But then, disaster struck.

Santa was performing his final checklist in the sleigh when Mrs. Claus hurried over, holding a small gift tag in her hand.

"Santa," she said, her voice tinged with concern, "this gift for Emily in Kansas says it's a soccer ball, but I peeked inside—it's a dollhouse."

Santa's eyes widened. "A dollhouse? That can't be right!"

Mrs. Claus handed him the tag, and he checked the logbook. Sure enough, Emily was supposed to receive a soccer ball.

"Oh, no," Santa groaned. "If one gift is wrong, how many others might be mixed up?"

Word of the mislabelled gifts spread through the workshop faster than a runaway sleigh. The elves froze mid-task, their cheerful chatter replaced with murmurs of panic.

Jingle, the head of logistics, burst into the room holding another mismatched tag. "We've got a problem! This gift for Tommy in New York says it's a train set, but it's actually a book about penguins!"

"Penguins?" Sparkle exclaimed, clutching a box of bows. "Tommy hates penguins!"

Grizzle stomped into the room next, holding up a package. "This was supposed to be a science kit for Lucy in London, but it's a pair of bunny slippers!"

The room erupted into chaos.

Santa clapped his hands, his deep voice cutting through the noise. "All right, everyone, calm down! We need to sort this out—and fast. We've got to make sure every child gets the right gift before the sleigh takes off."

Mrs. Claus nodded. "We'll divide into teams. Jingle, you and your group will recheck the gift tags. Sparkle, you take inventory and match gifts to the logbook. Grizzle, help reload the sleigh once everything is sorted."

"What about you, Santa?" Sparkle asked.

Santa adjusted his hat, determination shining in his eyes. "I'm going to help check every single gift. Let's move!"

The workshop became a flurry of activity.

Jingle and his team worked at lightning speed, examining each package and comparing the tags to the gift log. "This one's correct!" Jingle shouted, tossing a box into the "approved" pile. "This one isn't!"

Sparkle and her group scoured the inventory room, matching misplaced gifts to their rightful tags. "Found the soccer ball for Emily!" she yelled triumphantly, holding it up.

Meanwhile, Santa and Mrs. Claus went through the sleigh, double-checking each gift against the master list.

"Bunny slippers for Lucy in London?" Santa muttered, shaking his head. "Not on my watch."

As the hours ticked by, the team made steady progress. But the mix-up had created a ripple effect—some gifts were missing altogether, and replacements had to be made on the spot.

In the toy assembly department, elves worked overtime crafting new science kits, train sets, and even an emergency set of bunny slippers for a child who actually wanted them.

"We're running out of time!" Grizzle barked, lugging a crate of newly wrapped gifts toward the sleigh.

"We'll make it," Santa assured him, though he felt a twinge of doubt.

Finally, with less than an hour to spare, the last gift was loaded onto the sleigh. Santa wiped a bead of sweat from his brow as he inspected the neatly stacked presents.

"Is everything in order?" he asked, looking around at the exhausted but triumphant elves.

Jingle held up the checklist. "All gifts accounted for, and every tag matches the log."

"Excellent," Santa said, his voice filled with relief. "Now let's get this sleigh ready for take-off!"

As the reindeer were harnessed and the elves cheered, Santa climbed into the sleigh.

"Thanks to all of you, Christmas is back on track," he said, looking out at the crowd. "You've reminded me why this workshop is the best in the world."

Mrs. Claus handed him a thermos of cocoa and smiled. "Don't forget this, dear. You've earned it."

With a final wave, Santa cracked the reins, and the sleigh soared into the starry sky, leaving a trail of magic and glitter in its wake.

Back in the workshop, the elves collapsed into chairs, laughing and swapping stories about the day's chaos.

"You know," Sparkle said, "for a moment there, I thought we'd ruined Christmas."

Grizzle chuckled. "Nah. Santa always pulls it off—even if we give him a few extra challenges."

The room filled with laughter and the clinking of mugs as the elves toasted to another successful Christmas, proving once again that, no matter the obstacles, the magic of teamwork could overcome anything.

Chapter 17: Midnight Cocoa Club

At the North Pole, the days leading up to Christmas were always hectic, with the elves working around the clock to prepare toys, wrap gifts, and ensure everything was ready for Santa's big night. But amidst the chaos, a secret tradition flourished—a tradition known only to a select group of elves: the Midnight Cocoa Club.

The club wasn't official, nor was it sanctioned by Santa or Mrs. Claus. It began years ago as a way for overworked elves to blow off some steam, share stories, and enjoy a steaming cup of cocoa under the quiet glow of the northern lights.

On the night of December 22nd, Sparkle was the first to arrive at the hidden spot: a cozy nook tucked away behind the wrapping department's supply closet. The space wasn't much—a few old cushions, a battered table, and a string of twinkling fairy lights—but it was perfect for their clandestine gatherings.

She pulled out her flask of homemade peppermint cocoa and set it on the table, humming a soft carol to herself as she waited for the others.

"Am I late?" Jingle whispered, peeking around the corner.

"Nope, right on time," Sparkle said, grinning as he slid into the room, carrying a plate of gingerbread cookies.

One by one, the other elves arrived: Grizzle with his oversized thermos of "extra-chocolatey cocoa," Tinsel with a tin of marshmallows, and even tiny Sprinkle, who carried a mismatched collection of mugs.

"Okay, club members," Sparkle said as she poured the first round of cocoa. "Who's got a story for tonight?"

Grizzle leaned back against a cushion, cradling his mug. "I'll start," he said, a mischievous twinkle in his eye. "You know that giant teddy bear we made for the Johnson twins last week? Well, let me tell you what happened when I tested it."

The elves leaned in as Grizzle recounted his tale, complete with wild hand gestures and exaggerated voices.

"So there I was, face-to-face with this thing," he said, mimicking a dramatic pose. "I pull the activation string, and instead of saying, 'Merry Christmas,' it lets out this terrifying growl. Turns out, someone installed the wrong sound chip!"

The room erupted into laughter, cocoa sloshing in mugs as the elves doubled over.

Once the laughter died down, Tinsel spoke up. "That reminds me of the time the ribbon machine jammed and sprayed glitter everywhere. I had to dig myself out for twenty minutes!"

"Classic," Jingle said, shaking his head. "That machine's cursed, I swear."

"Speaking of cursed," Sprinkle piped up, her tiny voice cutting through the chatter, "remember the time Sparkle tried to make that glow-in-the-dark wrapping paper?"

Sparkle groaned, covering her face. "Please don't remind me. My hands glowed for a week. Mrs. Claus kept calling me her 'little firefly.'"

The room filled with laughter again, the warmth of the cocoa and the camaraderie making the workshop's stress melt away.

As the night wore on, the stories grew more whimsical.

"Did you know," Jingle began, lowering his voice for dramatic effect, "that there's a secret tunnel beneath the reindeer stables?"

"What?" Grizzle said, sitting up. "No, there isn't."

"There is!" Jingle insisted. "I found it last year when I was looking for my wrench. It leads to this tiny cave full of old Christmas decorations. I think it's where Santa keeps the retired sleigh bells."

"Now you're just making stuff up," Sparkle said, though she couldn't hide her grin.

"Am I?" Jingle said with a wink, sipping his cocoa.

As the clock struck midnight, the conversation took a softer turn.

"Why do you think we love Christmas so much?" Sprinkle asked, her small hands cupping her mug.

The room went quiet, the only sound the gentle crackle of the fairy lights.

"I think it's because it brings people together," Sparkle said after a moment. "Even when things are hard, Christmas reminds us that we're not alone."

The elves nodded, their smiles turning thoughtful.

"And cocoa," Grizzle added, raising his mug. "Cocoa definitely helps."

"To cocoa!" Tinsel said, and they all clinked their mugs together.

By the time the gathering broke up, the elves were yawning but content. They returned to their tasks with lighter hearts, ready to face whatever challenges the workshop threw their way.

Because at the North Pole, even in the busiest of times, there was always room for a little magic, a lot of laughter, and, of course, a steaming cup of cocoa shared among friends.

Thus ended another meeting of the Midnight Cocoa Club—a tradition as sweet and enduring as Christmas itself.

Chapter 18: The Reindeer Rebellion

With Christmas Eve fast approaching, the reindeer training sessions were in full swing. Every day, Santa's sleigh team practiced flying manoeuvres, emergency landings, and cargo weight adjustments under Rudolph's meticulous direction. But this year, the reindeer were feeling the strain more than usual—particularly Prancer.

Prancer wasn't known for complaining. In fact, he prided himself on being one of the most disciplined and graceful reindeer in the herd. But after weeks of gruelling workouts and a noticeable reduction in carrot rations, even Prancer's patience had its limits.

It started with a grumble during warmups.

"Another lap? Are you kidding me?" Prancer muttered, his breath fogging in the frosty air as the reindeer completed their third sprint down the snowy runway.

"It's necessary!" Rudolph called, trotting alongside the team. "We need to be ready for anything."

Prancer rolled his eyes. "Ready for what? Pulling a sleigh is the same every year. Why do we need all this extra training?"

"Because it's Christmas," Rudolph replied, as if that answered everything.

Prancer muttered something under his breath, but he kept running. For now.

By the end of the day, the reindeer were exhausted, their hooves dragging as they returned to the stables.

"That was brutal," Dasher said, flopping onto a pile of hay. "I'm not sure I've got another sprint in me."

"And where are the carrots?" Comet asked, poking his nose into the feed trough. "It's just oats again. We've had oats all week."

Prancer stood in the corner, his antlers gleaming in the dim stable light. "This isn't right," he said, his voice firm. "We work harder than anyone at the North Pole, and what do we get? Oats and overwork."

"What are you suggesting?" Blitzen asked, raising an eyebrow.

Prancer straightened. "I'm saying we deserve better. More carrots. Less exercise. And maybe a day off once in a while."

The other reindeer exchanged glances.

"Are you saying... we should strike?" Cupid asked hesitantly.

"Why not?" Prancer said, stamping a hoof. "Santa can't deliver Christmas without us."

The next morning, Santa was greeted by an empty runway and a neatly written note pinned to the stable door:

Dear Santa,

We, the reindeer, have decided to take a temporary break from training until our demands are met. We request:

More carrots.

A reduction in training hours.

A comfy new hay delivery for the stables.

Thank you for understanding.

Sincerely,

Prancer (on behalf of the Sleigh Team)

Santa read the note twice, his expression shifting from confusion to concern.

"Mrs. Claus," he called, waving her over.

Mrs. Claus read the note and chuckled. "I suppose even reindeer have their limits."

Word of the rebellion spread quickly through the workshop.

"The reindeer are on strike?" Sparkle exclaimed, nearly dropping a tray of ribbon spools. "Can they even do that?"

"I guess they can," Jingle said, grinning. "Good for them. Oats every day does sound rough."

Grizzle, munching on a cookie, added, "I say let them fight for their carrots. Everyone deserves a good snack."

Meanwhile, in the stables, the reindeer were enjoying their impromptu day off.

Prancer lounged in the corner, nibbling on a leftover carrot he'd hidden in his stall. "See? This is much better," he said.

"It is nice to have a break," Dasher admitted, stretching his legs. "But what if Santa gets mad?"

"Santa won't get mad," Prancer said confidently. "He's too jolly for that."

Santa, however, wasn't mad—he was determined.

"If the reindeer want more carrots, they'll get more carrots," he told the elves. "But we need to remind them how important they are to Christmas."

By mid-afternoon, Santa had organized a meeting with the sleigh team. He walked into the stables carrying a large basket of fresh carrots, their tops still green and fragrant.

"Prancer, Dasher, everyone," Santa said, his voice warm but firm. "I hear you loud and clear. You've been working hard, and I'm proud of you. But we're a team, and Christmas depends on us all working together."

He set the basket down, and the reindeer's noses twitched at the smell of the fresh carrots.

"Let's talk about your concerns," Santa continued. "I'll make sure you have enough carrots and some new hay for the stables. And we can reduce training hours slightly. But I need your commitment. Can I count on you?"

Prancer stepped forward, his head held high. "We appreciate the gesture, Santa. We just want to feel valued. If you promise to keep listening to us, we'll give it our all."

Santa smiled. "You have my word."

The reindeer exchanged glances, then nodded.

"All right," Prancer said. "We're back in."

By the time evening rolled around, the reindeer were back on the runway, their spirits lifted.

"Feels good to be appreciated," Comet said as he soared through the air.

"And the carrots were amazing," Blitzen added.

Prancer glanced at Santa, who waved from the sleigh below. "Maybe being part of a team isn't so bad," he admitted with a smile.

As the reindeer practiced their final manoeuvres, the North Pole returned to its usual harmony. The rebellion was over, the carrots were plentiful, and Christmas was back on track—thanks to a little compromise and a lot of heart.

Chapter 19: Santa's Fashion Fiasco

It was a quiet morning at the North Pole, just days before Christmas. The workshop hummed with its usual activity, and the smell of freshly baked cookies wafted through the air. Santa sat in his favorite armchair by the fire, reviewing his Naughty and Nice List, when Mrs. Claus walked in holding a stack of colorful fabric swatches.

"Nicholas," she began, her tone gentle but firm, "we need to talk about your suit."

Santa glanced up, adjusting his glasses. "What's wrong with my suit? It's been the same for centuries. It's perfect."

Mrs. Claus raised an eyebrow. "It's traditional, yes, but don't you think it's a little... dated? Red velvet, fur trim—it's lovely, but maybe it's time for something more modern."

"Modern?" Santa repeated, looking sceptical. "What's wrong with tradition?"

"Nothing," Mrs. Claus said, sitting beside him. "But imagine how the world would react if you showed up in something fresh, bold, maybe even trendy."

Santa stroked his beard thoughtfully. "Trendy, you say?"

The next day, Mrs. Claus enlisted the help of Sparkle, who had a knack for design, and Jingle, who had once declared himself the "self-proclaimed king of fashion."

They set up a makeshift design studio in the workshop, complete with sewing machines, fabric rolls, and mannequins. Santa sat on a stool, looking a little uneasy as the elves bustled around him.

"Let's start with something sleek," Sparkle suggested, holding up a swatch of shiny black fabric.

"Or bold!" Jingle countered, waving a piece of glittery gold cloth. "Nothing says 'festive' like sparkle."

Santa cleared his throat. "Can I at least keep the red?"

Sparkle sighed. "Fine, but we're updating the cut. No more baggy suits."

Hours later, the first design was ready. Santa stood in front of a mirror, examining himself in a sleek, tailored suit of crimson velvet with gold buttons and a matching sash.

"What do you think?" Mrs. Claus asked, her eyes twinkling.

"I feel like a maître d'," Santa grumbled, tugging at the sash. "What's wrong with my belt?"

"We're going for sophisticated," Sparkle explained.

"It's... something," Santa muttered.

The next outfit was even bolder. Sparkle and Jingle presented Santa in a shiny, sequined jacket with matching pants and a glowing LED trim.

"It's very... festive," Mrs. Claus said, trying to stifle a laugh.

"I look like a walking Christmas tree," Santa complained, spinning in the mirror. "How am I supposed to blend into the night like this?"

"Who said Santa should blend in?" Jingle said, gesturing grandly. "This is a statement."

"It's ridiculous," Santa muttered, ripping off the jacket.

The final attempt was Jingle's pièce de résistance: a slim-fitting jumpsuit in candy cane stripes, complete with knee-high boots and a matching red-and-white hat.

Santa stepped out of the dressing room, his expression a mix of embarrassment and annoyance.

"Absolutely not," he said before anyone could comment.

"You're no fun," Jingle huffed.

Mrs. Claus sighed. "Maybe we went too far."

By the end of the day, Santa was back in his chair, wrapped in his trusty red velvet coat and fur-lined boots.

"You know," Mrs. Claus said, sitting beside him, "your suit really is perfect the way it is. I just thought a change might be nice."

Santa smiled, taking her hand. "I appreciate the effort, my dear. But some things are better left unchanged."

Sparkle and Jingle popped their heads in. "So… no candy cane jumpsuit?" Jingle asked hopefully.

Santa chuckled. "Not this year, Jingle. But thanks for the laugh."

That Christmas Eve, Santa took to the skies in his classic suit, feeling more like himself than ever. And though his wardrobe didn't change, he appreciated knowing that even after all these years, his team still cared enough to make him shine—sequins or not.

Chapter 20: The Great Gingerbread Disaster

Every December, the elves looked forward to the North Pole's Annual Gingerbread House Contest. It was a chance for elves from all departments to show off their creativity—and indulge in a little friendly competition. This year, the stakes were higher than ever, with Mrs. Claus herself offering a golden rolling pin as the grand prize.

Excitement buzzed through the workshop as contestants assembled in the dining hall, where tables were piled high with supplies: freshly baked gingerbread panels, bowls of royal icing, gumdrops, candy canes, and sprinkles of every color imaginable.

"This is going to be the best contest yet," Sparkle said, rolling up her sleeves. She eyed Jingle, who was already stacking gumdrops with suspicious precision. "Don't think I haven't noticed your practice sessions, Jingle."

"I don't know what you're talking about," Jingle said innocently, though his smug grin suggested otherwise.

As the contest began, the dining hall transformed into a whirlwind of sugary chaos. Elves worked feverishly, piping icing, sticking candy in place, and occasionally sneaking a taste of the supplies.

Grizzle, ever the perfectionist, was carefully constructing a towering gingerbread castle complete with candy cane turrets and jellybean windows.

"You're all wasting time on decorations," he grumbled as Sparkle applied licorice shingles to her cozy gingerbread cottage. "Structural integrity is what counts."

"You say that every year, and you've never won," Sparkle shot back, laughing.

The first signs of trouble came when Sprinkle, the smallest elf, accidentally tipped over a bowl of powdered sugar. A cloud of white dust billowed across the room, coating everything—and everyone—in a fine layer of sweetness.

"Sorry!" Sprinkle squeaked, her cheeks turning as red as Rudolph's nose.

"It's fine," Jingle said, coughing and wiping sugar from his glasses. "Just a little ambiance, right?"

But the mishap seemed to set off a chain reaction.

Next, Tinsel's frosting bag burst mid-pipe, sending a jet of royal icing flying across the room. It landed squarely on Grizzle's half-finished castle, smearing one of his candy cane turrets.

"Hey!" Grizzle yelled, spinning around. "Watch where you're frosting!"

"It was an accident!" Tinsel protested, grabbing a towel to clean the mess.

Before the argument could escalate, a loud CRACK echoed through the hall. Everyone turned to see that Jingle's overly ambitious gingerbread skyscraper had collapsed, scattering candy rubble in every direction.

"No!" Jingle groaned, staring at the pile of broken cookies and crushed gumdrops.

"Too bad, Jingle," Grizzle said with a smirk. "I told you—structural integrity."

As the timer ticked down, the chaos reached its peak. Sparkle's licorice shingles began to slide off her roof, and Grizzle's castle tilted precariously to one side.

"I need more icing!" Sparkle shouted, frantically trying to reattach a wayward candy cane.

"Where's the gingerbread support beam I baked?" Grizzle muttered, searching under his table.

Meanwhile, Sprinkle was still sneezing powdered sugar, creating an almost magical snowfall effect that coated every gingerbread house in the room.

By the time Mrs. Claus called, "Time's up!" the room looked like a sugary battlefield. Broken candy and frosting smears littered the floor, and more than a few elves had icing in their hair.

Mrs. Claus walked slowly down the rows of gingerbread houses—or what was left of them—her expression a mix of amusement and bewilderment.

"Well," she said, trying not to laugh, "this is certainly... creative."

Grizzle's castle leaned so heavily to one side that it resembled a gingerbread version of the Tower of Pisa. Sparkle's cottage had lost most of its roof, leaving a sticky pile of licorice and icing on the table. Jingle's skyscraper was beyond repair, though he'd made a valiant effort to reassemble it into a "modern art installation."

The only entry that remained intact was Sprinkle's modest gingerbread igloo, which, while simple, had a certain charm.

Mrs. Claus clapped her hands. "The winner of this year's contest is... Sprinkle and her gingerbread igloo!"

The room erupted into cheers as Sprinkle stepped forward, her face glowing with pride.

"Congratulations!" Mrs. Claus said, handing her the golden rolling pin.

Sprinkle beamed. "Thank you! I just wanted to make something that wouldn't fall over."

As the elves cleaned up the sticky mess, they couldn't stop laughing at the day's mishaps.

"You know," Jingle said, wiping frosting off his glasses, "this might have been the most fun contest yet."

"Speak for yourself," Grizzle grumbled, though even he couldn't suppress a grin.

"Same time next year?" Sparkle asked, raising an eyebrow.

"Absolutely," Mrs. Claus said, chuckling. "But maybe with a little less powdered sugar."

Despite the disasters, the contest was a sweet success—a reminder that at the North Pole, even chaos could be deliciously fun.

Chapter 21: A Day in the Life of an Ornament Maker

In the bustling North Pole Workshop, elves were assigned to all sorts of departments—some crafted toys, others baked treats, and a select few worked in the Ornament Department. For Flicker the Ornament Maker, this was the ultimate honour. Ornaments weren't just decorative; they were tiny pieces of holiday magic meant to bring joy and sparkle to Christmas trees around the world.

Flicker's friends teased them about the "boring" job, but they didn't understand. Ornament-making wasn't just gluing glitter to glass; it was an art form. And today, Flicker was determined to prove it.

6:00 AM: The Morning Sparkle

The day began, as always, with a mug of cocoa and a checklist. Flicker stepped into the Ornament Workshop, where rows of tiny glass baubles gleamed under the soft glow of fairy lights.

"Let's see," Flicker murmured, scanning the schedule. "Snowflake ornaments for Norway, reindeer globes for Canada, and a special set of musical bells for the choir in Vienna. Busy day!"

Flicker tied on their apron—a patchwork of red and green with "Sparkle Specialist" embroidered on the front—and got to work.

7:00 AM: The Glassblower's Dance

The first step was shaping the ornaments. Flicker worked with a glassblowing elf named Blister, whose expertise was unmatched. Together, they transformed molten glass into delicate globes, twisting and shaping each one with precision.

"Careful," Blister warned as Flicker spun a glowing orb on the end of a long rod. "One wrong move, and it'll collapse."

"I've got it," Flicker said, their tongue poking out in concentration.

After a few tense seconds, the glass cooled into a perfect sphere. Flicker held it up, grinning. "Perfect!"

Blister nodded. "Not bad for a sparkle elf."

9:00 AM: Painting Magic

Next came Flicker's favorite part: painting the ornaments. They set up at their workstation, surrounded by tiny jars of paint in every imaginable color.

"Snowflakes first," Flicker said, dipping a fine-tipped brush into shimmering white paint. With careful, practiced strokes, they painted intricate snowflake designs onto each glass globe.

The designs had to be perfect. No two snowflakes were alike, and Flicker took pride in creating unique patterns for every ornament.

Halfway through, Sparkle popped her head in. "Still painting, Flicker? You've got the patience of a saint."

Flicker laughed. "It's not patience—it's passion. Now, don't distract me. This snowflake needs sparkle symmetry!"

11:00 AM: Glitter Explosion

As Flicker moved on to the glittering process, chaos struck. They had just opened a fresh jar of iridescent glitter when Grizzle wandered into the workshop.

"What are you doing here?" Flicker asked, eyeing him suspiciously.

"Just curious," Grizzle said, leaning over the table. "What's that stuff?"

"It's magic-grade glitter," Flicker explained. "Extra sparkly. Don't touch—"

Before they could finish, Grizzle accidentally knocked the jar over, sending a cloud of glitter into the air.

"Oh no," Flicker groaned as the glitter settled on their hair, apron, and even the floor.

Grizzle coughed, his face now sparkling like a disco ball. "Uh, my bad."

"Out!" Flicker shouted, grabbing a broom. "And don't touch anything on your way!"

1:00 PM: A Musical Challenge

The afternoon brought a special project: hand-tuning the tiny bells for the Vienna choir's ornaments. Each glass globe had a small bell inside that played a note when shaken. The challenge was tuning them to create a harmonious set.

Flicker sat at their station, tapping each bell with a tiny mallet and adjusting the metal clapper inside.

"Too sharp," Flicker muttered, tweaking one bell. "Now too flat."

After an hour of careful adjustments, the set was complete. Flicker shook the ornaments in sequence, and a cheerful tune rang out.

"Perfect!" they said, beaming.

3:00 PM: Quality Control Drama

As Flicker boxed up the finished ornaments, the Quality Control Team arrived to inspect their work. The lead inspector, Tinsel, was known for her sharp eye and even sharper tongue.

"Hmm," Tinsel said, holding up a snowflake globe. "This one's nice, but the glitter could be a little more even."

Flicker's stomach dropped. "What? Let me see!"

Tinsel handed it back, and Flicker inspected it closely. "It's symmetrical! See?"

"Barely," Tinsel said with a smirk. "But I'll let it slide. Great work, Flicker."

Flicker exhaled in relief. "Thanks, Tinsel. You're tough, but fair."

5:00 PM: Delivery Time

With the ornaments approved and boxed, Flicker loaded them onto the sleigh designated for international deliveries.

As the sleigh took off, Flicker felt a surge of pride. Every ornament they'd created would soon bring joy to families and brighten Christmas trees around the world.

"It's a lot of work," Flicker said, wiping glitter from their face. "But it's worth it every time."

That evening, as Flicker sipped cocoa in the breakroom, Sparkle sat down beside them.

"You know, I never realized how much goes into making ornaments," Sparkle said. "It's amazing."

"Thanks," Flicker replied, smiling. "It's not glamorous, but it's magical."

And as the workshop lights dimmed, Flicker knew they wouldn't trade their job for anything in the world. After all, nothing beat the feeling of creating tiny pieces of Christmas magic.

Chapter 22: When the Lights Went Out

The North Pole Workshop was in full swing, with elves bustling around as they worked tirelessly to finish toys, wrap gifts, and prep the sleigh for Santa's big night. The air buzzed with the sound of conveyor belts, cheerful chatter, and the occasional carol hummed by Sparkle, who always sang while she wrapped.

It was shaping up to be a perfect day until, without warning, the lights flickered once, twice, and then plunged the entire workshop into darkness.

"Uh... did someone just turn out the northern lights?" Jingle called from the wrapping department, his voice tinged with nervous laughter.

"Everyone stay calm!" Mrs. Claus said, her voice echoing through the sudden silence. "It's probably just a minor glitch."

But the workshop wasn't built for "minor glitches." Within seconds, chaos erupted.

"Where's the emergency lanterns?" Sparkle asked, fumbling around in the dark.

"They're in the supply closet," Tinsel replied, her voice muffled as she tripped over a box of ribbons. "I think."

"Great, and where's the supply closet?" Jingle added, bumping into Sparkle with an "Oof."

In the toy assembly department, Grizzle's booming voice cut through the confusion. "Everyone, stop touching things! You'll mess up the inventory!"

"But I can't see anything!" a panicked elf replied.

"That's the point! Just... don't move!"

Meanwhile, Santa and Mrs. Claus huddled in the workshop's control room, where the emergency power system was supposed to kick in. Santa squinted at the control panel, trying to make sense of the blinking red lights.

"What does this one mean?" he asked, pointing to a button labelled Power Failure Level 2.

"It means the workshop's out of juice," Mrs. Claus said, rolling up her sleeves. "We need to get the backup generator running."

The backup generator, unfortunately, was located in the basement—a place notorious among the elves for being dark, cold, and full of creaky pipes.

Sparkle, Jingle, and Grizzle volunteered to find it, armed with nothing but flashlights and a vague map drawn by a very forgetful elf.

"This place is creepy," Sparkle whispered as they descended the stairs.

"It's just pipes and shadows," Jingle said, though he stuck close behind her. "Totally not haunted or anything."

Grizzle snorted. "Haunted? It's a basement, not a gingerbread graveyard. Keep moving."

Back in the workshop, Rudolph decided to lend his glowing nose to the wrapping department. He trotted in, his bright red light illuminating piles of half-wrapped presents.

"Rudolph!" Tinsel exclaimed. "You're a lifesaver!"

"Just doing my part," Rudolph said, glowing a little brighter with pride.

"Great," Tinsel said, handing him a roll of tape. "Now hold this and don't move. You're our only light source!"

Down in the basement, the generator hunt wasn't going well. The trio stumbled over tangled wires and stacks of forgotten equipment, their flashlights casting long, eerie shadows.

"This is ridiculous," Grizzle grumbled. "Why isn't this thing labelled?"

"I think I found it!" Sparkle shouted, pointing to a large machine covered in cobwebs.

"Finally," Jingle said, brushing off the dust. "Now, how do we turn it on?"

Grizzle inspected the machine, his brow furrowed. "Looks like it needs a crank."

"A crank?" Sparkle repeated. "What is this, the 1800s?"

As the elves struggled to get the generator running, Santa and Mrs. Claus tried to keep the workshop calm.

"We've handled worse," Mrs. Claus said, patting Santa on the arm. "Remember the snowstorm of '82? No lights, no heat, and half the reindeer came down with the flu?"

Santa chuckled. "You're right. This is nothing compared to that."

Still, he glanced out at the darkened workshop and sighed. "But it would be nice to get the lights back on soon."

In the basement, the trio finally found the crank, which was inconveniently hidden under a pile of old elf-sized boots.

Grizzle grunted as he turned the handle, the generator sputtering to life. The machine groaned, coughed, and then roared into action, flooding the basement with a faint hum of power.

"Yes!" Sparkle cheered. "We did it!"

"Great," Jingle said, catching his breath. "Now let's get out of here before this thing decides to explode."

When the lights flickered back on in the workshop, a cheer erupted. Elves hugged, high-fived, and clapped Rudolph on the back for his glowing service.

Santa and Mrs. Claus exchanged relieved smiles as the conveyor belts hummed to life again.

"Good work, team!" Santa called, his voice carrying across the room. "Let's get back to making magic!"

As Sparkle, Jingle, and Grizzle returned to the workshop, covered in dust and cobwebs, the elves greeted them like heroes.

"What took you so long?" Rudolph teased.

"Oh, you know," Sparkle said with a grin. "Just saving Christmas."

By the end of the day, the workshop was back on schedule, and the power outage was already becoming a favorite story among the elves.

"Maybe we should label the generator next time," Sparkle suggested.

"Or invest in something that doesn't require a crank," Jingle added.

Santa laughed. "One thing's for sure—we can handle anything as long as we work together."

And as the elves returned to their tasks, the hum of the workshop felt brighter than ever.

Chapter 23: Mrs. Claus's Spa Day

With only a few days left until Christmas, the North Pole Workshop was operating at full speed. Elves darted between departments, the conveyor belts hummed, and the scent of peppermint cookies wafted through the air. In the midst of it all, Mrs. Claus stood in the kitchen, rolling out dough for her famous sugar cookies.

She wiped her forehead with the back of her hand and sighed. "I don't know how much more of this I can take."

Santa looked up from his list-checking station. "What's wrong, my dear?"

"I've been baking, organizing, and stitching for weeks," she said. "I think I need a break."

"A break?" Santa repeated, startled.

"Yes, Nicholas," she said firmly. "A day off. I'm going to the North Pole Spa, and you're in charge until I get back."

Santa waved as Mrs. Claus boarded the sleigh that would take her to the spa, her face already looking more relaxed.

"You'll be fine without me, won't you?" she asked, raising an eyebrow.

"Of course!" Santa said, puffing out his chest. "How hard can it be?"

As soon as the sleigh disappeared into the snowy horizon, Santa turned to the elves. "All right, team. Let's get to work!"

The trouble began almost immediately.

In the kitchen, Santa attempted to finish the batch of cookies Mrs. Claus had started. He rolled out the dough too thick, creating lopsided shapes that barely resembled trees and stars.

"Don't forget the timer!" Sparkle called from the doorway.

"Timer?" Santa said, looking confused.

The timer was already beeping when Santa finally remembered it. He opened the oven to find half-burnt, half-raw cookies staring back at him.

"Well, these have... character," Santa muttered, dumping the tray into the sink.

Next, Santa moved to the Wrapping Department.

"How hard can it be to wrap presents?" he asked Jingle, picking up a roll of glittery wrapping paper.

Ten minutes later, Santa had taped his beard to a package, wrapped a box upside-down, and somehow managed to tangle himself in a roll of ribbon.

"Maybe leave the wrapping to the experts," Jingle suggested, trying not to laugh.

Santa nodded, brushing glitter off his suit. "Good idea."

Things weren't any better in the Sleigh Maintenance Bay.

"Rudolph, can you check the harness straps?" Santa asked, attempting to sound confident.

Rudolph gave him a sceptical look but complied.

Meanwhile, Santa tried to polish the sleigh. He accidentally used a jar of glitter glue instead of wax, leaving the sleigh with a sticky, sparkly coating that refused to come off.

"Santa," Dasher said, inspecting the mess, "I don't think Mrs. Claus is going to like this."

"Don't tell her," Santa said, wiping his hands on a towel.

Back at the spa, Mrs. Claus was enjoying the most peaceful day she'd had in years. She soaked in a peppermint-scented hot tub, sipped cocoa topped with whipped cream, and listened to soft carols played on a harp.

"This is heaven," she murmured, her worries melting away.

By late afternoon, Santa was overwhelmed. The kitchen was a disaster, half the workshop was covered in glitter, and the sleigh was still sticky.

"I don't know how she does it," Santa admitted, sinking into his chair.

"She's Mrs. Claus," Sparkle said with a smile. "She's magic."

Santa nodded. "I just hope I can clean all this up before she gets back."

When Mrs. Claus returned that evening, she found the workshop eerily quiet.

"Nicholas?" she called, stepping into the kitchen.

She froze, taking in the burnt cookies, glitter-covered counters, and a sheepish Santa standing in the middle of the chaos.

"I can explain," Santa said quickly. "I might have underestimated how much you do around here."

Mrs. Claus smiled, shaking her head. "I hope you've learned your lesson."

"I have," Santa said sincerely. "And I'll make sure you get a spa day every year from now on."

That night, as they sat by the fire, Mrs. Claus handed Santa a cup of cocoa.

"You're lucky I love you," she teased.

"I know," Santa said, chuckling. "But maybe next year, you could leave a guidebook?"

Mrs. Claus laughed. "We'll see, Nicholas. We'll see."

And as the snow fell gently outside, the North Pole returned to its usual rhythm—this time with a well-rested Mrs. Claus at the helm.

Chapter 24: The Lost List

The morning of December 23rd started like any other at the North Pole. Santa was in his study, reviewing the Naughty or Nice List one final time. The massive scroll detailed the names of every child in the world, their deeds meticulously recorded by the elves. It was the cornerstone of Christmas—without it, Santa couldn't deliver the right gifts.

But when Mrs. Claus brought Santa his morning cocoa, she noticed something unusual.

"Nicholas," she said, glancing at the desk, "where's the List?"

Santa froze, his hand halfway to his cocoa. "It's right... oh no."

The Naughty or Nice List was gone.

Panic set in immediately. Santa flipped through the papers on his desk, checked under the cushions of his armchair, and even looked inside his cocoa mug. Nothing.

"It must be here somewhere!" Santa exclaimed, pacing back and forth.

"Calm down, dear," Mrs. Claus said, placing a comforting hand on his shoulder. "We'll find it. Let's retrace your steps."

Santa summoned the elves, and soon the workshop was buzzing with activity. Sparkle, Jingle, and Grizzle were put in charge of the search party.

"Where were you last with the List?" Sparkle asked Santa, holding a notepad to jot down clues.

"I was here in my study," Santa said. "But then I took it to the Wrapping Department to double-check some names."

"Let's start there," Jingle said, leading the group.

The Wrapping Department was in its usual state of organized chaos, with elves frantically tying bows and stacking boxes. The team searched every inch of the room, from under the ribbon spools to inside the tape dispensers.

"Nothing here," Grizzle said, shaking his head.

"Wait!" Sparkle exclaimed, holding up a candy cane with scribbled notes on it. "Is this part of the List?"

Santa squinted. "No, that's my grocery list. I needed marshmallows."

The search continued.

Next, the group moved to the Reindeer Stables, where Rudolph was supervising a harness fitting.

"Santa, did you bring the List in here?" Rudolph asked, his nose glowing faintly.

"I don't think so," Santa said, scratching his beard. "But I did stop by to check on the reindeer."

The elves searched the hay bales, the feed bins, and even under the sleigh parked in the corner.

"Found it!" Jingle shouted, holding up a rolled-up piece of parchment. But when he unrolled it, the page read:

"To Santa: Practice your landings! - Dasher"

The team groaned. "Still no List," Sparkle said, her shoulders sagging.

As the hours ticked by, the search grew more frantic. The elves checked the kitchen, the toy assembly line, and even the Snowflake Filing Room, where the records of past Christmases were kept.

Finally, Santa clapped his hands. "Stop!" he said. "I remember now—I took the List to the Candy Department to verify the candy cane inventory!"

The team hurried to the Candy Department, where Sprinkle was overseeing a batch of peppermint bark.

"Have you seen the List?" Sparkle asked, out of breath.

Sprinkle tilted her head. "A big scroll? Oh, I saw it this morning. It was on the counter."

"And where is it now?" Jingle asked urgently.

Sprinkle pointed to a towering pile of candy boxes. "It might be under there."

The elves dove into the stack, tossing candy canes and chocolate bars aside as they searched. After several tense minutes, Sparkle let out a triumphant yell.

"I found it!" she cried, holding up the Naughty or Nice List.

Santa rushed over, taking the scroll and unrolling it carefully. "It's all here," he said, his voice filled with relief.

The workshop erupted into cheers as the team returned the List to Santa's study, placing it securely on his desk.

"I'll keep a closer eye on it this time," Santa promised, tucking the List into a special drawer.

"You'd better," Grizzle said, dusting off his hands. "We're too close to Christmas for another crisis."

That night, as the elves sipped cocoa and shared stories of the day's chaos, Santa raised his mug in a toast.

"To teamwork," he said, smiling at the group. "And to never losing the List again."

The room filled with laughter and clinking mugs. And as the snow fell softly outside, the North Pole Workshop returned to its usual buzz, ready to make this Christmas the best one yet.

Chapter 25: The Great Elf-Off

At the North Pole Workshop, there was one thing elves loved more than cookies, cocoa, and carolling: competition. Whether it was ribbon curling, candy cane balancing, or ornament decorating, the elves thrived on friendly rivalries. But this year, the workshop was buzzing with anticipation for the biggest event yet: The Great Elf-Off.

The challenge? A toy-assembling showdown to determine the fastest, most skilled elf in the entire workshop.

The contenders were Sparkle and Grizzle, two of the workshop's most talented—and competitive—elves. Sparkle was known for her precision and flair, while Grizzle prided himself on efficiency and speed. Their rivalry had been simmering all season, and the Elf-Off was the perfect opportunity to settle the score.

"I hope you're ready to lose, Sparkle," Grizzle said, cracking his knuckles as he stood at his workbench.

"Lose?" Sparkle replied with a smirk, adjusting her apron. "I'm about to make toy history."

The rules were simple: assemble as many toys as possible in one hour. Each toy had to pass quality control, and any mistakes would result in a penalty. The winner would receive the coveted Golden Wrench, a gleaming trophy that had been displayed prominently in the workshop all week.

Elves from every department gathered to watch, filling the room with cheers and chatter. Santa and Mrs. Claus sat in the front row, eagerly awaiting the showdown.

"Let the Great Elf-Off begin!" Santa boomed, raising a candy cane like a flag.

The timer started, and both elves sprang into action.

Sparkle immediately got to work on a dollhouse, her hands moving with the precision of a master craftsman. She painted tiny shutters, glued miniature furniture into place, and sprinkled glitter onto the roof.

Meanwhile, Grizzle chose to assemble a toy train, snapping wheels and tracks together at lightning speed. "Efficiency, not glitter," he muttered under his breath, casting a sidelong glance at Sparkle's sparkly dollhouse.

"Quality over quantity," Sparkle replied without looking up.

The first ten minutes were neck and neck. Sparkle finished her dollhouse just as Grizzle completed his train. Both passed the quality check with flying colors, earning cheers from the crowd.

But as the challenge wore on, their strategies began to diverge. Sparkle focused on intricate toys like tea sets and rocking horses, while Grizzle churned out simple items like bouncy balls and wooden blocks.

"She's wasting time on details," Grizzle muttered, assembling another train.

"Better than cutting corners," Sparkle shot back, carefully painting stripes onto a toy zebra.

At the halfway mark, disaster struck.

Sparkle accidentally knocked over a jar of glitter, creating a sparkling mess that covered her workstation. "No, no, no!" she cried, frantically brushing glitter off her tools.

Grizzle, seeing his opportunity, smirked and sped up his pace. "Looks like the queen of glitter is in trouble."

But karma wasn't far behind. Moments later, Grizzle's conveyor belt jammed, sending a pile of unfinished trains crashing to the floor. "What? No!" he groaned, scrambling to fix the jam.

The crowd roared with laughter and cheers, delighted by the unexpected drama.

As the clock ticked down to the final minutes, both elves pushed themselves to their limits. Sparkle's glitter mishap didn't stop her from completing a fully decorated carousel, while Grizzle recovered from his conveyor belt fiasco to churn out a fleet of toy airplanes.

"Ten seconds left!" Mrs. Claus called, her voice barely audible over the cheers.

Both elves raced to finish one last toy. Sparkle glued the final piece onto a doll's dress, while Grizzle snapped the wings onto an airplane just as the timer buzzed.

The room fell silent as Tinsel, the head of quality control, stepped forward to tally the scores.

"Let's see," Tinsel said, inspecting the toys. "Sparkle, you completed 14 toys. Grizzle, you finished 16."

Grizzle let out a triumphant whoop, raising his arms in victory. "I knew it! Efficiency always wins."

"Hold on," Tinsel said, raising a hand. "Grizzle, one of your airplanes is missing a wheel, and one of your trains has a loose track. That's two penalties."

Grizzle's smile faltered as the crowd murmured.

"That means Sparkle wins with 14 perfect toys!" Tinsel announced, holding up the Golden Wrench.

The crowd erupted into cheers as Sparkle stepped forward to accept the trophy.

"Well played, Sparkle," Grizzle said, shaking her hand. "But next time, I'm double-checking everything."

"Looking forward to it," Sparkle replied with a grin.

As the elves celebrated, Santa and Mrs. Claus smiled at each other. The Great Elf-Off had been a success, proving once again that a little friendly competition—and a lot of teamwork—made the North Pole brighter than ever.

Chapter 26: Rudolph's Diary: Life in the Spotlight

December 10th

Sometimes, I wonder if anyone understands what it's like to be me—Rudolph the Red-Nosed Reindeer, the most famous sleigh navigator in Christmas history. Don't get me wrong, I'm grateful. My glowing nose has helped save Christmas more times than I can count. But being a legend? That's not as easy as it looks.

Take today, for example. I was just trying to enjoy my carrot breakfast when a group of elves ran up, cameras in hand. "Rudolph!" one of them squealed. "Can you stand by the Christmas tree for a picture? We need a new calendar cover!"

I sighed but obliged. By the time they were done, my breakfast was cold, and Dasher was laughing at the glitter they'd stuck to my nose.

Fame comes with its price.

December 12th

The team's been training hard for Christmas Eve. I love flying, but lately, it feels like everyone's watching me, waiting for me to do something amazing.

"You've got it easy, Rudolph," Blitzen said during a break. "You don't even have to try anymore. That nose does all the work."

Easy? If only he knew. Sure, my nose lights up, but I also have to be the first one in line during a blizzard, scanning the skies for chimneys and storm clouds. I'm not just a reindeer—I'm a beacon, a map, and a flashlight rolled into one.

December 15th

Today, Mrs. Claus pulled me aside for a chat.

"You've been looking stressed, dear," she said, patting my nose gently. "Are you all right?"

I didn't want to complain, but I admitted I was feeling the weight of expectations. "Sometimes, I think everyone just sees the nose, not me," I told her.

She smiled kindly. "Your nose may be special, Rudolph, but it's your heart that makes you shine. Don't forget that."

Her words stuck with me all day. Maybe being Rudolph isn't so bad after all.

December 18th

Another day, another round of fan mail. Sparkle brought me a sack of letters, most of them from kids who wanted to know how my nose works.

One letter stood out. It was from a boy named Charlie who said he sometimes feels left out at school because of his glasses. "You're my favorite reindeer," he wrote. "You make me feel like it's okay to be different."

I stared at that letter for a long time. Maybe being in the spotlight isn't just about the pressure—it's about showing others they can shine, too.

December 22nd

Training went better today. I decided to stop worrying about what the others think and focus on doing my best.

"You were on fire out there!" Comet said after our final run.

"Literally," Dasher joked, pointing at my glowing nose.

I rolled my eyes but laughed anyway. Sometimes, you just have to embrace the jokes.

December 24th

It's Christmas Eve, and the air is electric with excitement. Santa gave us his usual pep talk, but this time, he singled me out.

"Rudolph, I couldn't do this without you," he said, placing a hand on my shoulder. "You remind us all what it means to shine, no matter the weather."

As we took off into the night, the clouds parted just enough for the moon to peek through. My nose lit the way as always, but this year, I felt lighter—like I wasn't just a light for Santa's sleigh, but for everyone watching from below.

December 25th

Another Christmas complete. As I lay in my stall, surrounded by the quiet hum of the North Pole, I felt a sense of peace.

Being Rudolph isn't always easy, but it's worth it. Because if my nose can light the way for Santa, maybe it can light the way for others, too.

Here's to another year of flying, shining, and finding joy in being me.

Chapter 27: Snow Day Shenanigans

The morning started like any other at the North Pole Workshop—elves rushing to complete last-minute toys, reindeer practicing their take-offs, and the smell of Mrs. Claus's cinnamon rolls wafting through the air. But as the day progressed, the skies darkened, and the snow began to fall.

At first, it was light and picturesque, the kind of snowfall that made the North Pole sparkle. But within an hour, the wind picked up, and the gentle flurries turned into a full-blown blizzard.

"Attention, everyone!" Santa's voice boomed over the workshop's intercom. "Due to the snowstorm, the workshop is officially closed for the day. Stay warm, stay safe, and we'll resume tomorrow!"

The elves froze, unsure of what to do. A day off? That never happened!

"Did he just say we're closed?" Sparkle asked, blinking in surprise.

Jingle grinned. "You know what that means—snow day!"

Within minutes, the elves were bundled up and heading outside, leaving their workstations behind. The snowstorm may have stopped the workshop, but it wasn't going to stop the fun.

Snowball Battle Royale

The first order of business was a snowball fight. Jingle, Grizzle, Sparkle, and Tinsel divided into teams and immediately began building fortresses out of snow.

"You're going down, Sparkle!" Grizzle shouted, lobbing a snowball that narrowly missed her.

"Not if I get you first!" Sparkle retorted, expertly tossing a snowball that hit Grizzle squarely on the hat.

The battle raged for nearly an hour, with elves dodging, diving, and laughing so hard they could barely throw straight. In the end, Sparkle's team declared victory after a well-aimed snowball from Tinsel toppled Grizzle's fort.

Reindeer Sleigh Races

Meanwhile, the reindeer decided to host their own event: sleigh races. Rudolph and Dasher teamed up against Prancer and Cupid, pulling small sleds with elves cheering them on.

"Faster, Rudolph!" Sparkle yelled as she held on tight.

"I'm trying!" Rudolph called back, his hooves kicking up snow.

In the end, Prancer and Cupid won by a nose—though Dasher claimed it was because "Rudolph's glow distracted him."

Snow Elf Sculpting

As the storm began to ease, Sparkle and Jingle decided to hold a snow elf sculpting contest. The goal was simple: create the best snow elf using only what you could find in the snow.

Sparkle crafted an elegant snow elf with candy cane arms and gumdrop buttons, while Jingle's creation was more abstract, resembling a snowman with extra-long legs.

"What is that supposed to be?" Sparkle teased.

"Art," Jingle replied with mock seriousness.

Mrs. Claus arrived to judge the sculptures and declared Sparkle the winner. "But Jingle gets points for creativity," she added with a wink.

Hot Cocoa Finale

As the sun began to set, the elves returned to the workshop, where Mrs. Claus had set up a hot cocoa bar. Steaming mugs of cocoa were topped with whipped cream, marshmallows, and sprinkles, warming everyone after their snowy adventures.

Santa joined them, chuckling as he surveyed the scene. "I don't remember the last time we had a snow day," he said, raising his mug. "You've all earned this break."

As the snowstorm finally subsided and the North Pole settled back into its usual rhythm, the elves couldn't stop talking about their impromptu day off.

"It was the best snow day ever," Sparkle said, sipping her cocoa.

"Let's do it again next year," Jingle suggested.

"Let's not," Grizzle grumbled, brushing snow out of his ear.

But even he couldn't deny that the snow day had brought a little extra magic to the North Pole—and reminded everyone that sometimes, the best memories are made when things don't go as planned.

Chapter 28: Elf Tech Support

The North Pole Workshop was a marvel of tradition and innovation. Elves still crafted wooden toys by hand, but over the years, technology had made its way into Santa's operations. Nowhere was this more evident than in Santa's sleigh, which had recently been upgraded with a state-of-the-art GPS system designed to make navigating Christmas Eve's complex route easier.

But while the sleigh was cutting-edge, Santa was anything but tech-savvy.

"Techie!" Santa's voice boomed across the workshop, echoing with urgency.

Techie the elf, head of the North Pole's Tech Support Department, froze mid-sip of his peppermint latte. "Uh-oh," he muttered, setting down his mug.

Moments later, Santa strode into the Tech Support Room, clutching the GPS manual. His face was flushed with frustration.

"This thing," Santa said, waving the manual like it was a naughty list offender, "is impossible!"

Techie sighed but kept his smile. "Okay, Santa, let's start from the beginning. What seems to be the problem?"

"The problem," Santa said, sitting down heavily in a chair, "is that it keeps talking to me! Every time I press a button, it says something about recalculating or rerouting. I just want it to show me the next house!"

Techie nodded, pulling up a chair. "That's the voice assistant, Santa. It's meant to help you stay on track."

"Well, it's not helping!" Santa said, crossing his arms. "And what's a 'recalculation'? I never had to recalculate with my paper maps."

Techie powered up the GPS unit and opened the interface. "Okay, Santa, here's how it works. The GPS calculates the best route based on your starting point, destination, and weather conditions. If you stray off course—like, say, to grab an extra cookie—it'll recalculate to get you back on track."

Santa frowned. "What if I don't want it to recalculate? What if I already know the fastest way to Timmy's house?"

"Then you ignore it," Techie said with a shrug.

Santa raised an eyebrow. "Ignore it? Doesn't that defeat the purpose?"

"Well... yes," Techie admitted. "But it's there to assist, not take over."

Techie spent the next hour walking Santa through the basics of the GPS: entering destinations, adjusting the volume of the voice assistant, and switching between aerial and sleigh-level views.

"This button zooms in," Techie explained. "And this one zooms out."

"Why would I want to zoom out?" Santa asked.

"To see the big picture," Techie replied patiently.

"I already have a big picture," Santa said, gesturing to his mental map. "It's called 'knowing the world.'"

By the time they moved on to advanced features, Santa's frustration was bubbling over.

"What's this blinking icon?" Santa demanded, pointing at the screen.

"That's a weather alert," Techie said. "It tells you if there's a storm ahead."

"Do I really need a machine to tell me about storms? I have Rudolph for that!"

Techie stifled a laugh. "Rudolph's great, but the GPS can help with route adjustments if the storm is severe."

Santa grumbled something under his breath but didn't argue further.

Finally, Techie set up a practice run for Santa. They loaded a test route into the GPS, complete with simulated obstacles like chimney backups and weather delays.

"Okay, Santa," Techie said, handing him the controls. "Follow the instructions on the screen."

Santa squinted at the screen as the voice assistant chirped, "Turn left at the next candy cane marker."

"Left?" Santa muttered. "But I always go right around Candy Cane Lane."

"Just try it," Techie encouraged.

Santa reluctantly followed the instructions, and to his surprise, the simulated route shaved off five minutes.

"Well, I'll be," Santa said, stroking his beard. "Maybe this thing isn't so bad after all."

By the end of the day, Santa was navigating the practice routes with surprising ease.

"You've got the hang of it now," Techie said, smiling.

"Thanks, Techie," Santa said, clapping the elf on the back. "But if it starts recalculating for no reason on Christmas Eve, I'm calling you at midnight."

Techie laughed. "I'll keep my radio on, just in case."

As Santa left the Tech Support Room, Mrs. Claus stopped by to check on the progress.

"How'd it go?" she asked, sipping her cocoa.

"He's getting there," Techie said, grinning. "But I think he'll always prefer his instincts over technology."

"Some things never change," Mrs. Claus said with a chuckle.

And as the workshop lights dimmed, Techie returned to his desk, ready for whatever Christmas tech challenges came next. Because at the North Pole, even Santa sometimes needed a little extra guidance.

Chapter 29: A Christmas Eve Miracle

The stars glittered in the night sky as Santa's sleigh soared above the snow-covered world. Christmas Eve was in full swing, and the reindeer team was running at top speed, expertly guided by Rudolph's glowing nose. Elves back at the North Pole watched the sleigh's progress on their tracking map, cheering every successful delivery.

But as Santa approached a small, snowbound village in northern Canada, something went terribly wrong.

"Hold steady!" Santa called to the reindeer as they began their descent. The blizzard below was fierce, but Santa trusted his team. They'd flown through worse before.

As the sleigh landed, the snowdrifts proved deeper than anticipated. The runners sank into the powdery ground with a groan, and when Santa tried to move forward, the sleigh wouldn't budge.

"Dasher! Prancer! Pull harder!" Santa urged.

"We're trying!" Dasher called back, his voice strained.

The sleigh didn't move an inch. It was stuck.

Back at the North Pole, the tracking system flashed an alert.

"What's going on?" Sparkle asked, leaning over the map.

Jingle squinted at the blinking red light. "It looks like Santa's sleigh has stopped moving."

"Stopped moving?" Grizzle said, peering at the screen. "On Christmas Eve? That's bad. Really bad."

Mrs. Claus entered the room, her face calm but serious. "We need to find out what happened—and fast. Sparkle, open the radio line to Santa."

"Santa, are you there?" Sparkle's voice crackled through the sleigh's radio.

"I'm here, Sparkle," Santa replied. "We've got a problem. The sleigh's stuck in a snowdrift, and we can't get it out."

The elves exchanged worried glances.

"What can we do to help?" Sparkle asked.

"Send backup," Santa said. "We need something to pull us free."

Within minutes, the workshop was a whirlwind of activity. Sparkle, Jingle, and Grizzle loaded a smaller rescue sleigh with tools, ropes, and a fresh team of reindeer. Mrs. Claus prepared a thermos of extra-strong cocoa for Santa, while Techie double-checked the rescue sleigh's GPS to ensure they wouldn't get lost in the storm.

"Let's move!" Sparkle shouted, climbing into the rescue sleigh.

The team took off, the wind biting at their faces as they flew into the blizzard.

When the rescue team arrived, Santa was pacing beside his stuck sleigh, his boots sinking into the deep snow.

"Took you long enough!" Dasher called, panting from the effort of trying to pull the sleigh free.

"Hang tight," Sparkle said, hopping out of the rescue sleigh. "We've got this."

The team worked quickly. Jingle and Grizzle tied ropes to the sleigh's runners while Sparkle connected them to the rescue sleigh's harness. Rudolph and the other reindeer stood by, their breaths forming clouds in the freezing air.

"Ready?" Sparkle called.

"Ready!" the team shouted back.

"Pull!" Sparkle yelled, and the combined strength of both sleigh teams strained against the ropes. The stuck sleigh groaned, its runners creaking as they shifted in the snow.

"It's moving!" Rudolph shouted, his nose glowing brighter in excitement.

"Keep pulling!" Santa urged, his face lighting up with hope.

With one final heave, the sleigh broke free from the drift, sliding smoothly onto firmer ground. Cheers erupted from everyone, their voices ringing out over the howling wind.

Santa clapped Sparkle on the back, his eyes twinkling with gratitude. "You saved Christmas, Sparkle. I don't know what I'd do without you."

"It's a team effort, Santa," Sparkle replied, grinning. "But you owe us cookies when we get back."

"Done," Santa said, laughing.

With the sleigh back in action, Santa and his team resumed their journey, delivering gifts to the small village and beyond. The rescue team flew alongside them for a while, making sure everything was running smoothly before heading back to the North Pole.

By the time the sleigh returned home, the sun was rising, and the workshop erupted into cheers. The elves celebrated with mugs of cocoa and plates of cookies, their spirits high despite the long night.

Later, as Santa and Mrs. Claus sat by the fire, Santa raised his mug in a toast.

"To the best team in the world," he said. "And to the miracles that happen when we work together."

And as the North Pole settled into its well-deserved rest, the magic of Christmas shone brighter than ever—proof that even in the toughest moments, teamwork could save the day.

Chapter 30: The Day After Christmas

The North Pole was unusually quiet on the morning of December 26th. For the first time in weeks, the workshop's conveyor belts were still, the reindeer were snoozing in their stalls, and the elves were lounging in the breakroom, sipping cocoa and munching on leftover cookies. The rush and chaos of Christmas had passed, leaving behind a cozy calm.

Santa sat in his favorite armchair by the fire, his boots off and his feet propped up on a footstool. Mrs. Claus brought him a steaming mug of cocoa, laced with extra marshmallows.

"You deserve a rest, dear," she said, settling beside him with her knitting. "It was another magical Christmas."

Santa smiled, a deep chuckle rumbling from his chest. "Magical, yes, but not without its challenges. That snowdrift in Canada nearly did us in."

In the workshop breakroom, the elves were swapping stories of their favorite—and not-so-favorite—moments from the season.

"Remember the glitter wrapping paper disaster?" Sparkle said, grinning. "I think we're all still finding glitter in our hair."

Grizzle groaned, brushing a stray sparkle from his sleeve. "I'll never look at glitter the same way again."

"And what about the Great Elf-Off?" Jingle chimed in, pointing at Sparkle. "You're officially the fastest toy assembler at the North Pole."

"Don't forget my flawless victory," Sparkle teased. "Though Grizzle gave me a run for my money."

Meanwhile, the reindeer were lounging in the stables, swapping their own tales of Christmas Eve.

"That blizzard was no joke," Rudolph said, shaking his head. "But we pulled through."

"Barely," Dasher replied, nibbling on a carrot. "Santa better give us double carrots next year."

Cupid stretched out on a pile of hay. "I just want a day off with no sleigh bells ringing in my ears."

Back in the main hall, Mrs. Claus gathered everyone for their annual post-Christmas meeting. Santa joined her, looking rejuvenated after his morning cocoa.

"All right, team," Mrs. Claus began, smiling warmly. "Another Christmas is behind us, and it was one for the books. You all worked tirelessly to make it happen, and we couldn't have done it without each and every one of you."

The elves and reindeer cheered, their exhaustion momentarily forgotten.

"But now," Santa added, his eyes twinkling, "it's time to talk about something just as important: our vacation!"

The room erupted in excited chatter. Vacation planning was a tradition at the North Pole—a well-deserved reward for months of hard work.

"I vote for a tropical island," Jingle said. "I'm ready to trade snow for sand."

"Mountains," Grizzle countered. "Nothing beats a cozy cabin and hot cocoa."

"What about a reindeer retreat?" Rudolph suggested. "A place where we can stretch our legs without worrying about sleigh drills."

Sparkle laughed. "I'm fine with anywhere that doesn't involve wrapping paper."

Mrs. Claus jotted down the suggestions, promising to come up with a plan that everyone would love. In the meantime, she announced, the elves were free to spend the next week however they pleased.

As the meeting ended, the team scattered, some heading back to their rooms for a nap, others brainstorming vacation ideas over a second helping of cookies.

That evening, as the North Pole settled into its rare moment of quiet, Santa and Mrs. Claus sat by the fire, reflecting on the season.

"Another year done," Mrs. Claus said, sipping her tea. "And another year of memories."

Santa nodded, gazing at the crackling flames. "It's not just the gifts we deliver that make Christmas special—it's the magic we create together. Even when things go wrong, it's those moments that remind us what this season is all about."

Mrs. Claus smiled. "Here's to another year of Christmas magic—and maybe a few less mishaps."

Santa chuckled. "But what would the holidays be without a little chaos?"

And so, as the elves and reindeer dreamed of sandy beaches, snowy peaks, and well-deserved rest, the North Pole settled into its post-Christmas calm—content, fulfilled, and ready for whatever adventures the next year would bring.

Disclaimer

The stories, characters, and events in The North Pole Diaries: Secrets of Santa's Workshop are entirely fictional and meant for entertainment purposes only. While this book aims to spread holiday cheer and a sense of magic, it does not claim to depict the actual workings of Santa's Workshop (which, of course, remain a closely guarded Christmas secret). Any resemblance to real-life elves, reindeer, or jolly old men in red suits is purely coincidental.

This book contains humour, light-hearted mischief, and whimsical illustrations that may cause uncontrollable laughter or an irresistible urge to bake cookies. Reader discretion is advised: side effects may include a heightened belief in holiday magic and an overwhelming desire to spread joy.

Keep the spirit of Christmas alive, but please don't hold us responsible if your glitter supply mysteriously runs out after reading.

Milton Keynes UK
Ingram Content Group UK Ltd.
UKHW031045291124
451807UK00001B/95